# DREAMS ARE ONLY THE BEGINNING

*Becoming who you were meant to be*

*Original Text - 2002*
*Revised - 2007*
*Revised - 2009*

BY DOROTHY A. MARTIN-NEVILLE
PHD, DCEP, EMP.

## Dedication

This book is dedicated with great love and gratitude
to the new generations of dreamers
including Michael, Amy, Lee, Madison,
Kaitlyn, and Colin.

# Contents

# Introduction

Dreams for my future have been the driving force of my life. They have kept me alive, kept me sane, and allowed me to go from surviving to living. I have come to see dreams as an absolutely necessary aspect of life. They are what separate those who are getting through the day from those who are creating each and every day of their lives. Have you lost touch with your life force? Your passion? Your self? If so, these qualities are easier to reclaim than you may think. To transform your life, on every level, from survival to living, just allow yourself to dream. You will discover that your life is limited only by your ability to dream, and, by your willingness to take the risks necessary to follow those dreams, whether big or small.

Recognize that your life, at this moment, is a reflection of the choices you have already made. You have painted the portrait of who you would become even if at times you gave that privilege and that power to someone else out of fear, loneliness, or a belief that you didn't truly know what was inside of you and calling you to become more, to become what it is your are here to become. If you did give it all away or simply didn't claim that freedom, one of the greatest choices you can make for yourself right now is to start anew, to define the present and the future according to the dreams and choices you make for yourself from here on out. Allow yourself to dream and to dream big - outrageously, and without limit.

Starting my life in a "home for children," as my mother called it, being adopted, and growing up as an Irish Catholic girl in the housing projects of South Boston, Massachusetts, I created a series of dreams, one step at a time, that would take me to places and situations I never could have imagined. After leaving the projects, I became a Catholic nun, a Trans World Airline stewardess, a wife, a mother, a single parent, a licensed psychotherapist, a graduate-school teacher, the founder of The Institute of Healing Arts and Sciences, LLC, (IHAS), a Clinical Instructor at The University of Connecticut Medical School, an author of three books, lecturer, and TV and radio guest in several countries. Amazingly, that was only the beginning....

Many only allow their dreams to surface superficially and usually only during long winters or in the midst of an insane schedule. Some of us are more lenient, and allow our dreams to surface, fully, and to be lived completely. When they are so strong, they demand to be heard. How many of you have thought of dropping everything and moving to a far off exotic land? How many of you have done it?

After dropping the younger of my two children off at college, I returned home, sobbing the whole way, knowing that it was time for the next step in my own journey, but not knowing what that was. What I knew was that for a kid from the projects, a large four bedroom colonial was a huge, lonely place to be in all by yourself. It was certainly too big for me. I was over 40, the kids were gone, and now it was my turn. After thinking for a short while, and remembering a dream I had years before, when the kids were small, I picked up the phone and called a real estate agent to put my house on the market. I then called American Airlines to buy a one way ticket to Anguilla, BWI, in the Caribbean, six miles northeast of St. Martin. Over the next two weeks, I notified my patients I was leaving the country and referred them to other therapists if needed. It became clear to me at that point, and has remained so, that there is no limit to what we can dream, if we only let ourselves.......

Those successful dreamers we read about or see on television are not superhuman or even any more special than you or I. They are simply people who stood up and said, "I have a dream." We can easily become one of that chosen group. The greatest quality they possess, something we all have, is courage - courage to risk it all and to follow their hearts and their souls. Courage is not the choice to live without fear but a choice to not let fear stop the movement forward. Someone once said to me, as I was going through a divorce, "You are the most courageous woman I have ever known." I was stunned because I was filled with fear and I told him so. He said, "If you didn't have fear, you wouldn't have courage, you wouldn't need it. You are you in spite of the fear. That is courage."

I guess I have lots of it, although I have heard others call it less complimentary names. I have realized over time, however, that courage, when blended with humor, faith, and hope allows us to live our lives fully. With joy, laughter, tears, and endless hope, nothing seems too difficult for long or too outrageous. If you can dream it, you can make it a reality, so start dreaming and just follow the path. What you discover is that at the end, and during the process, there is always you, a you that you never knew existed. One that makes you proud, feel alive, and grateful for the journey. What a gift that is!

Let me tell you my story. It is the story of a woman who began life in an orphanage and was raised in the housing projects. Instead of getting married right after high school graduation as I had dreamed, a new dream developed and I moved to the safety and the freedom of the convent. After that dream, there begins a journey of travel as an international airline stewardess, marriage, parenting, divorce, international lecturing, and romance. This story entails all the awareness I have gained as a therapist as well as all the fears, pains, and hopes that are part of being a woman in transition. Although it is *my* story, it is also the story of so many who have left behind "surviving" and risked coming alive and living life to the fullest and from the heart. I hope, for you, it provides a guideline, or at least an understanding, of what can be required and yet allow you to see how totally worth it, and exciting, the journey becomes when you follow your dreams.

The original version of this book ended several years ago when I lived on Anguilla, BWI. Much has happened since then and, as a result, some of the original dreams have been fulfilled while others have run their course and been replaced by those dreams which have called me forward to the next stage of the unfolding journey. I invite you to travel with me, and to explore your journey as well, encouraged to know your dreams and to make them all come true, if you choose.

# Chapter One
## Childhood

*Our family is where we come from
and it helps make us who we are.
It is there that we learn to dream -
sometimes just to survive.*

WHEN I WAS GROWING UP IN THE 1950's, South Boston, or "Southie" as it was known to those of us who lived there, was a little island filled mostly with Irish Catholics. Many were proud of that fact. God made people, and then He made the Irish. According to my dad, the best Irish were the Boston Irish. The Irish in all the other major cities of the USA were all competing to be second place, yet they would always be far behind those from Southie. The folks in "the old country" were just farmers, waiting to become one of us, which was why every week more kept coming in. My family, my little part of this community, consisted of my mom, my dad, my older brother Bob, myself, my sister Mary Catherine, who we called May, my brother Joe, and my littlest brother Jimmy. Dad had wanted 20 children but mom couldn't have more than five so that is where it stopped. Back then, "Thank God" was all I could say about that. We had more than enough to take care of as it was and bedroom space was limited. Now, I would love the idea and would cherish more brothers and sisters. They are a gift beyond words who to this day add to my life immeasurably even though we live far apart.

To help you better understand the dynamics of our little family, let me begin at the beginning and tell you a little something about my parents and their childhood. It explains a lot. My dad was born out of wedlock to a French waitress and an Irish sailor. After birth, he was placed in a box and put on the church steps, for anyone to take. He was temporarily placed in an orphanage until an elderly Irish/German couple took him in since they had no children of their own and she had always wanted a child. As he grew, my dad proved to be quite a handful. Listening to him, you can just picture this poor old Irish woman running down three flights of stairs because he would threaten to throw himself under a bus or a horse drawn cart if she didn't give him money or do whatever else it was that he wanted. My grandmother worked nights cleaning floors in an insurance company that, during the day, would not allow the Irish or blacks to work in the corporation itself. They could only clean the building that housed it.

When my dad was eleven, his mother died and, as a result, his father, who had been a very sick, angry, violent German man, was placed in long-term hospital care. A local Irish family, the Lynches, took my dad in but at 15 he forged his birth certificate and joined the merchant marines. He longed both to get away and to find adventure in WWII. Once he was in the war, however, it was clear he was still a child in many ways. He speaks from a child's perspective of hiding under the bunks when action took place on the destroyer he was assigned to. He became a Boiler Maker 1st class before leaving the military, getting a job as a sheet metal worker when he got out.

My mom's family history was quite different. She came from a home that was a blend of her dad, a flamboyant Irish Catholic immigrant, well over six feet tall with typical red hair, and her mom, who was less than five feet tall and of proud old New England stock – originally Irish - from New Hampshire. My grandmother conceived almost 20 children but lost most at or around the time of birth. Only 5 made it to adulthood and only 3 besides Mom, two aunts, and one uncle, lived long enough to meet all of us. My grand-father worked as a longshoreman on occasion and on the trains at other times, depending on who fired or laid him off last. As many Irish men do, I hear he loved to sing, laugh, party, and drink his brew. Depending upon which aunt you talked to, you could hear many varied stories of the family. The bottom line seems to be that my mom was the most vibrant, powerful, and popular of the children and she was also the youngest girl.

My mother married at 17 for a very brief period after conceiving my brother Bob. She left her husband in the army in Georgia and moved back in with her mother in Boston. After a couple of years, my mother fell in love with another man, and eventually become pregnant. Because his family disapproved, they never married. As a result, this child was considered by my grandmother to be illegitimate. Because of her Catholic standards, my grandmother would not allow an illegitimate child to live in her home. My mother was forced to make a choice of staying with her mother and giving up the illegitimate child or getting her own apartment and raising her two children alone. She chose to stay with her mother and, as a result, I was placed in an orphanage.

Two years later, my mother, pregnant again, would remarry and have a third child. This new man, who became my dad, having been in an orphanage himself as an infant, chose to take me from the orphanage and adopt both myself and my older brother, raising all 5 children as his own. My father thought he found the family he had never really had and my mom thought she had found stability and possibly prosperity. Their dreams, and their realities, were unfortunately far apart to begin with and things only grew worse.

In marrying my dad, my mom moved out of her mother's home, although she brought her mother with her, and into a housing project apartment that would be filled with violence and rage. Although she was a very intelligent and powerful woman, my mom was raised to believe that as a woman she was weak and that she could not survive without someone, especially a man, around. She would pay a high price for that belief. Living on her own and making a successful career was too modern a concept - beyond my mom's understanding - so she stayed in this second marriage. She used to tell me her mother always said, "If you make your bed, you sleep in it." What a sad and hopeless statement....

Dad later talked of coming home drunk late at night on the back of fire engines while ringing the bell. (The Irish tended to be cops or firemen in those days.) Eventually his drinking stopped but not the behavior. Although neither will talk about it, I am sure that very early on they realized their dreams would never be realized. My dad wanted that happy, warm family he had never had, yet he never realized he had to create it from love and understanding - it didn't just happen. My mom wanted success and a chance for a better life, yet she had no idea how to make that happen. She became a Republican while he was a staunch Democrat. In South Boston, a working class neighborhood at best, that was a major statement. They came from different worlds and had very different dreams and yet still they were both looking to be loved. Mom was young when she had her 5 children and her dreams of the better life were moving further and further away as the demands on her and her time kept increasing. Dad worked two or three jobs just to pay the bills and his disappointment and hopelessness came out as rage, making all of their dreams impossible.

In the beginning, dad was a sheet metal worker and mom was a telephone operator. Eventually she became a waitress and then a reservations agent for Trans World Airlines which caused problems in our home because now she was meeting and enjoying many different types of people. People who very different from dad. She was too embarrassed to bring them home into our house in the projects or to have them meet dad and, as a result, her two worlds never joined. They were just too different.

As we got older, it was clear that dad was a hard-working man. He became a policeman, took a lot of side jobs called "details" to make more money, and later took a third job delivering alcohol at night after work. He was taking risks and earning more money for the family while she was beginning to experience life outside of Southie as never before. With all the increased income, however, things never really seemed to get better. With five children growing and needing more clothes, food, and other expenses, it just never seemed to be enough. They both were aware, as well, that they walked in different circles and with different dreams. Mom wanted a life, very middle class if possible, for all of us combined with travel. Dad wanted Southie, a few close friends and total control. My father's increasing feelings of frustration and inadequacy came out as greater violence towards all of us. If he felt threatened or inadequate, power and being in control seemed to be the answer. As a result, our home was filled with fear, anxiety, depression, and rage with immense hurt and fear on all sides. So often it felt like a train wreck waiting to happen. With no one having any idea of how to get it under control, it just kept going faster and faster.

It was such a complicated mix for a child to understand. He was very hard working and generous with his family yet he was brutal and raged filled. She was an extremely powerful, hard working woman, who believed she was powerless in her relationship with my father while all the while being trapped in a social level far below what she felt she deserved. She reminded me often that we were better than these people. These people who threw food out their windows, who talked trash, and who wore dirty clothes.

She told me you may not have many clothes but they can always be clean. She wanted better and believed she and we deserved better. She had that with her friends at work, yet she came home to us, to dad, and to the projects. It was more than my mom could handle. While dad filled with rage, she became more depressed. She struggled and tried to survive, physically and emotionally, while being hospitalized periodically and getting away from it all. I was the oldest daughter and the most outspoken. In my mind's eye, because of mom's sadness and her belief in her powerlessness, it was my job to become the one who contained dad, protected the family, and picked up where my mom left off. It all made sense to me because I often felt that although she was with us physically, emotionally she was somewhere else, perhaps in her better world. Someone needed to take an active role or it would be a ship without a captain. Someone needed to find a way to make smooth sailing, to soothe the wounds, and to bring us together as a family.

As a result, I developed a sixth sense very early. As the oldest girl, and the one with the most power in the house, next to my father, I felt responsible for the others. I could tell when my father had turned onto our street. I never knew how I knew; I just knew that dad was almost home, I could feel him. This level of High Sense Perception was a spiritual gift I didn't understand. I thought everyone had it. I just knew things. I would run around to make sure all the beds were made, everything was cleaned up, dinner was started, and the kids were all behaving. No matter how hard I tried or what I accomplished, there was always something he could find to be angry about. The phone might ring, or someone may be sitting too close to the television, and that would cause the beatings to start. If you cried and screamed that you hadn't done anything that day, then you were being beaten to be reminded of who was in charge and what would happen if you did do something wrong tomorrow. Nothing was ever good enough to just be loved or even acceptable.

Until the day I die, I will remember, as if it was yesterday, the sound of a belt coming out of a man's pants. I will remember the argument my parents had over whether or not my dad could beat us up with an open or closed fist or whether a belt was better. I remember Joe having his face shoved in his plate of food when he said something wrong at the dinner table. I remember Bobby being beaten in his bedroom because he had entered a friend's apartment when no one was home. He and some friends had eaten cookies. He was a good kid and he did something wrong. It wasn't vicious or malicious, just wrong. Yet the punishment never fit the "crime" because any opportunity to let out brutality and rage was taken by my dad. He never missed an opportunity; he even created some. Still, perhaps because of the level of brutality, the viciousness, in this assault, I couldn't believe my mom and all of us stood outside that door listening for what felt like forever when all I wanted to do was kick the door in and beat up my dad to make him stop. I wanted to make the screams and the cries, the sounds of violence go away. Dad was so big. Bob was just Bob, my big brother. I never realized you could love and hate someone so fully at the same moment - and my mom just stood there...

I felt so powerless, so overwhelmed, and so sad that often I just wanted to die. Nobody did anything about any of this. This was just life here on this earth, waiting and wondering who would get beaten next while inside I was screaming to be held, to be touched gently, and to be enjoyed, not tolerated or beaten. Sometimes I was even too numb to feel fear. Sometimes I just survived, hopeless. If mom wasn't going to do anything, how were we going to survive? How were we going to get out, get away, make it stop? For whatever reason, I just took my dad as being hopeless and helpless. He was who he was. I didn't think of him changing, only of us escaping with my mom in the lead. Perhaps I sensed she had more to her, more ability, more knowing, if only she would touch it and use it, for herself and us. I also came to see, as an adult, that I came to never really expect much from men at all. I saw them all as similar to my dad, stuck, hopeless, and limited as human beings. I could settle for feeling loved, if only they could show me that. It was all I needed. I would do the rest. I didn't consider them capable of having any ability to grow or to change. As a result, with Dad, I remember wondering if I would ever make it out alive. I remember wondering, as well, if I would make it out sane. I had a vision as a child, which lasted for years, of me sitting in a rocking chair in the cold stark basement of an insane asylum - wrapped in a straight jacket and just rocking and rocking and rocking for all my days here on earth, never being able to understand the "why."

Throughout my teens and into my thirties, I had a reoccurring nightmare. It took place in the projects. Everyone was being gathered from all the buildings, all the families. We were made to walk, one at a time, into these booths where electrical currents were sent through our brains and when we came out we would all be good, we would all behave, and, we would all be half dead. A few people had to go in twice. They kept sending me through time and time again but I kept holding on to a part of me -to a part of my soul, my independence, my being – and they kept making me go back inside. They could see that I still had life in me, passion, will and desire. I couldn't understand why the others gave up so quickly. Did they really have so little life force or was I just too dumb or too stubborn to know better? I was terrified because I could feel my resistance falling a little bit more each time I passed through. I was so terrified I would lose it, lose the will to exist as me. I would wake up filled with terror and go to sleep terrified that that nightmare would come again, and even more so, that this time I would be gone forever. My dad used to say that they break the wild spirit in horses and he was going to break me in the same way, for my own good.

Knowing he wanted to, and that he might succeed, I started to dream. I had to get out, to escape, to be free and to feel loved. I needed to believe it was possible. I dreamed a doctor in the emergency room would adopt me. I dreamed that this time dad would break a bone and I would need to go to the hospital. That way, the doctor would meet me and decide to adopt me right there. As I sat with it, I became terrified for my family. What would happen to them if I were not around? Who would help them? Who would talk to dad for them? I couldn't leave them but I could dream about it.

In the meantime, I needed my mom, but she was just too overwhelmed with all the children and such an emotionally charged home. Perhaps she could have managed if it was just the children, but she was too terrified to try. She always said children needed a father but I believed, even more so, she needed a husband. I remember her getting up every morning and making lunches for herself and us and then doing the initial preparation for dinner. She would peel the potatoes, make the meat loaf, and put a can of vegetables out for Bob or I to cook before she and my dad got home, so dinner would be ready at a "reasonable hour." As I see it, her life was filled with struggle, fear and regret - fear of never getting out of South Boston and fear of my father. Regret for never having accomplished her goals for a better life because she got pregnant so early and so often, and regret at the marriages she chose. I believe that because I was now the outgoing one, the one with the vibrancy and power, even thought I felt terrified inside, that I reminded her of herself as a child, more so than any of the others. She had let those great qualities go into hiding and lived her life in survival while I was living them fully and getting into trouble because of them. In her eyes, she saw me duplicating her life and I think she was just waiting for it all to happen to me. I believe she sensed that I had "something"; she just believed I would never take the opportunity to discover what that was. She felt that same sense of helplessness and hopelessness towards my life that she had for her own. I remember her telling me that I had a great heart but no substance and therefore would get no place in life unless I was very lucky. Mary, who was the good, quiet one, would amount to something because she used her brains in school and behaved. I got into trouble. I had great grades, it came easy, but the back of the card was another story. They said I couldn't take credit for the brains, God gave those to me, but the big mouth was all mine. She felt I would never amount to anything because I was "boy crazy." I believe, that was how she saw her life, but thankfully, it was not to be mine.

Unbelievably, my mother and my father have always said I was his favorite. I came to believe that was because, at that time, I was the only one who really had any semblance of a relationship, or connection, with him. I was the only one who would relate to him in any way at all. The others were too frightened or just didn't want to. She also knew I could stop my dad, if anyone could, or at least tone him down. She would tell the others, "Have Dottie talk to your dad." I was the powerful female in this house, not her. I was also the girl who at 10 was hospitalized with a potential ulcer and who in high school was treated for acute anxiety. The job I had taken on, because she wouldn't or couldn't, was more than a young girl could handle, more than anyone could handle.

Sadly, my mom had no idea how to connect on an emotional level with me. I remember clearly, asking her one day, when I felt so estranged, if she loved me at all and she said, "I have to, you're my daughter." I accepted on that day the kind of relationship we would have. As a result, there was an emptiness I didn't know if I could ever fill. I was about 12 and knew I would need to do this on my own and so I did. She would not be there for me. Perhaps it was her guilt. She had also told me that she was afraid of me. Whatever the cause, she couldn't hold and comfort me and tell me it would be OK; she didn't believe it. For so many years after that, I felt so alone and so isolated. I did it alone even in a relationship. I didn't rely on others to support me or even turn to them. I took things on by myself, never trusting others could or would want to help me. I believed that she had a special connection with each of the others and then there was me, her oldest daughter. Bobby was her first, and her favorite, and they came into this together. Mary was sickly and a good girl, Joe was "different" and needed her, and Jimmy was the baby. She provided for me as much as for the others. She always wanted to be fair and love us "all the same," as she would say. Yet every relationship with a child is different even if the care is the same. Ironically, my life has been the exact opposite of hers, and Mary has followed her to a tee. It is the family joke, that Mary and Mom have lived the same journey, from the number of husbands to the jobs they and their husbands held, through their lives. May and Mom have both been married three times, both their second husbands were policemen and both Mom and Mary worked in airlines reservations. I became the risk taker, the one who broke away and the one who lived a life far different than theirs. I believe I have lived the life my mother may have lived in a different place or time.

As alone as I felt, thankfully, my brothers and sister were always there. They are great. They are a lifeline and provide a grounding sense of continuity and connection for me. Let me introduce them to you. Bob, who is four years older than me, was quiet and found solace in his books. He was terrified of my dad and had no idea how to handle him, so he read or stayed out of the house. Bob was, and is, a gentle soul who just wanted peace. He loves nature, paints, rides his bike, and just loves great food and great wines. He was my big brother and I thought he was the smartest guy in the whole world. I adored him. He was also the safest man I knew. He was not at all affectionate but I knew he understood. It was a shared knowing we never really talked about but which we experienced.

He and I were in this together. It was as if we were one generation and the other kids were the next. We saw it all so differently than they did, or, at least we thought so. They seemed like kids and we felt like very old survivors. To this day, I think of Bob with such love and gratitude just for being my brother. He can be very serious and I bring laughter and outrageousness into his life. I trust we will always be there for each other.

Bob has spent his adult life in service. Soon after college he was a newspaper reporter in Massachusetts. He also taught high school in Massachusetts but left that to teach at the American College in Zambia. Initially, he enjoyed it but over time different problems arose. He also came to realize that many of the students who he taught were going back to South Africa and were being killed. Educated blacks were a threat. It was as if he was preparing them for death. That along with other things caused him to return to the states suffering from the results of malaria. After working for prisoner legal representation, doing political work and writing a couple of books, he worked in public health and is now in hospital administration. Although we have taken different paths, there is an amazing similarity in our careers. We have both taught, have both worked in the medical field in varying capacities, and have both been published. We are definitely family. I know he loves and admires me, especially my willingness to take risks. He is the only family member who has ever come to one of my speaking engagements and that seems so appropriate. We were out there together as kids, adopted together, and saw each other in a different light and we still do.

The next child is Mary, my only sister. Mary was very ill at birth and almost died. Consequently, she was always considered the fragile one. Dad would say, "Someone sneezes in China and Mary catches the cold." She had a number of illnesses as a baby and yet thankfully she made it. I really thought of her as my little sister even though there is only a two year difference in our ages. At one point in time, we slept in a double bed and whenever I heard my dad coming in I would lie across Mary to protect her so that I could take the blows from the belt and not her. He didn't care who he hit as long as he could get his point across, whatever it was. Even when I was mad at her because she was always the good one, the one the Sisters told me I should be like, I felt she needed my protection and I would give it. I remember when she was about 8, she told me she was praying for my soul because she saw me kissing a boy on the lips. She knew I was going to go to hell and she was trying to save me. I guess she tried to save my soul and I tried to save her body. My parents needed a good girl and a bad girl so we filled the bill, even later, when we completely reversed roles. Mary did *good girl* better than I and she did *bad girl* better than I did as well. She's gifted. She does nothing half-way. Mary jumps in with both feet.

I love my sister totally and unconditionally. We never judge each other at this point. We may get annoyed at times but we have been through too much in our lives to point a finger at one another. When one goes "overboard," the other points it out, but in love. We have been through divorces, kids, relationships, parents, and so much more. She lives her life loving others, whether it's all her grandchildren or through her participation in her local 12-step program. May (her nickname) brings her love and message to women in prison as well as to so many lucky folks she sponsors. She is a woman filled with love and gratitude and thankfully humor because it sure is needed. I have two things over my desk that she has given me over the years and I read them daily. One says, "God made us sisters but we made us friends." The other is a needlepoint that says, "A sister is someone special to love." May is definitely someone special. She has lived through so much and yet her caring for others continues to grow. Her desire to love keeps spreading.

Joe, the next youngest, is one year younger than May. He is a man with a great heart and an unbelievable sense of humor. I am well aware that many men who come from violent homes become violent men. All of my brothers have turned out to be gentle loving souls with great generosity and a desire for intimate connection on a heart level. What a blessing! He was the kid who one Christmas took a bite out of every chocolate in the box of chocolates we got. He was sent to his room but he took the chocolates with him. He forgets that story but I admired him and was furious at him at the same time. I never would have thought of that. He was a smart guy and could work the system, usually. No wonder he went into politics later.

He was also the opposite of what my dad wanted. Dad wanted a jock he could encourage along, someone he felt he would know how to parent. Joe is a tall, thin gay man who has been much more at home in the political arena and now as someone heavily involved in movies and TV, behind the scenes. He is a treasure. Because he has no kids of his own, he is a phenomenal uncle to all his nieces and nephews. His humor and honest enjoyment of who they are make him a wonderful uncle to have. He is so unconventional that they feel completely at home with him even if he is of another generation, and yet, he clearly expects them to live up to who they are, however they choose to do that. Because he refused, as a child, to follow in my father's footsteps, he was punished and humiliated often. Thankfully, he developed coping skills that have allowed him to be who he has become. My mom said for years that we are like five points to a star. We are all so different from each other yet so intrinsically a part of one another.

Jim, who is two years younger than Joe, is the youngest. He was like my baby. I carried Jimmy around on my hip. He and I were extremely close when he was little. I gave him the love and affection we all needed. It was me he came to, to be changed or held. I loved having someone to cherish who could cherish me back. I took his name in religious life. I was Sr. James Marie. That way I felt that I was keeping a part of him with me. Being the youngest, Jimmy had many years at home alone, after we had all left. He grew up in a different family in some ways, because by that time my mother had another husband. Jim is still my little brother although he is the one who would visit May and I each year when we were both divorced with little ones and fix anything and everything that needed fixing in our respective homes. He has tried to take care of us "since men should do that for a woman." He is a mixture of traditional gallantry and an obnoxious brat and he is quite proud of the blend. He is the wonderful completion of a group of brothers and sister who learned to stick together early and who haven't forgotten.

For whatever reason, I didn't understand as a child, I felt I was emotionally and physically stronger than the others, except dad. Because of my love for my brothers and sister, it was so much harder for me listening to or seeing him beating the others because I feared they would be killed or emotionally destroyed. Somehow, at those moments, I never felt that would happen to me, so I would take him on. While the others hid or cried, I would scream and tell him I hated him, and that they hadn't done anything wrong. He would let my mother or brothers or sister go and then start on me. At times, when I could do it, I would get him infuriated because I refused to cry. I refused to give him that power.

The hook that got me and kept me in a permanent state of confusion with him was that although on some level I hated my dad for all that he did to us, I also pitied and loved him. When he wasn't enraged over something, he was a vulnerable little boy wanting the warm loving family he never had. He couldn't understand why he didn't have it. There was no ability to connect cause and effect; no realization that the parent needed to let the children feel the warmth and safety first, then they would climb on your lap. He had no understanding that if a child approached you to read a story whether you felt like it or not, out of love, you treasured this child and took the moment to give all the love you had and also that you received so much more than you gave.

Fortunately, life wasn't all beatings, there were other times; the beatings just overshadowed everything else because they were daily and without apparent provocation. On Fridays, we would get tuna grinders, or spuckies as they were called in Southie, mine with lots of pickles and oil. As Catholics we couldn't eat meat on Fridays but rather than being a sacrifice it was a special treat. It was either that or clam cakes, but those required a long walk to City Point to buy them at a special store. Spuckies (Grinders, hoagies in other parts of the country) with potato chips were definitely better and so much more fun. Every summer Dad would save all his coupons from Stop & Shop and we would go to Nantastic Beach Amusement Park. It was the high point of our summer vacation. Having the nerve to ride the big roller coaster signified one huge step in growing up.

Throughout his life, Dad's generosity remained. He took great pride and joy in his ability to give us whatever bit he had in his pocket. On Sundays, if dad had the money, we got ice cream cones at the local store. Sodas cost a nickel then so if we had saved any money from lunches during the week we really lived it up, or, even better, we could get a bag of penny candy that could take hours to eat. There were so many things that you could get at 4 for a penny and those were usually what we got, or, "buttons" which were sheets of paper with little colored sugar drops on them that looked like buttons. Over the years I have gone out and bought some of those "fantastic" goodies. Oh my God, are they awful... (Growing up can sure change things, such as your taste buds.) Still, life could be pretty good. With a little chalk you could play hopscotch all weekend and with a pimple ball you could play points until dark every day, as long as no one was sitting on the front stoop. Once the balls were flat, we would cut them in half and use a broomstick to play half-ball, similar to baseball. Life could be fun with imagination.

In its own wonderful way, "Southie" was like every other ethnic neighborhood in the 50's in that it had its own unique character. You can feel the energy of an ethnic neighborhood: it pulsates as you walk through it. There is no place in the world like it, whatever the nationality. There is life-force energy, a vibrancy, that is all its own. Because this one was Irish Catholic, it had its own stories. If your parents didn't send you to hell, the nuns, the priests or the church would; consequently, a part of every Saturday afternoon was spent in confession. If you didn't have any sins, you made some up because, as Sister said, "only God is perfect." If you thought you hadn't sinned this week you MUST have forgotten something because no one went a whole week without sinning. I remember being 8 years old and confessing "impure thoughts." Who knew? It was better to confess too much than not enough because the forgotten ones could get you into hell or 40 lifetimes in purgatory. Also, most of us spent a lot of time saying certain phrases that got family or friends 30, 60, or 90 days off their time in purgatory if they had died already. As far as we were concerned, the Church still had control over your afterlife.

Superstition was also a way of life. You never opened an umbrella in the house, or walked in the path of a black cat, or under ladders. If you started the rosary at night and held it under your pillow while praying, the angels would finish it for you if you fell asleep. If you dreamed of someone who had died, it was their way of telling you they needed some more prayers to get out of Purgatory. (Doesn't it make you wonder why now they are having trouble believing that those on the other side walk with us daily when before they talked to us so readily?) Family was about, keeping family members out of hell, getting them out of Purgatory faster or, if alive, at least keeping them out of trouble with their parents, the nuns, and the police. It kept the rest of us out of trouble too because we were so busy praying. Someone knew what they were doing… In the past few years, I must have watched the movie *Moonstruck* 15 times. I loved it, so I own it. Although they were Italian, not Irish, they were still Catholic, and very ethnic. She was a good girl with a wild side, great credentials for a woman. They were crazy. Things didn't have to make sense, they just were. In some ways it was all so simple then. Everyone knew the rules and everyone knew everyone.

In those days, although it was the projects, and you could readily get beaten up, you could still leave your scooter out all night and it was safe. Your things were safe, just you weren't. We had our priorities. When we were younger very few people had cars so life was all within walking distance. As adolescents we could take the bus to downtown Boston, or, even walk if we chose and had the time. For fun, at night we sometimes had block parties where we would hang Christmas lights around the front stoop, play a record player, and dance. Those were more of the fun times and Ruthie, the lady upstairs, made her popcorn. We all knew everyone and it was a time to celebrate the weekend or the summer or a birthday, whatever. Dancing and music made it all special and life seemed easier and less stressful at those times. They brought everyone together in a peaceful way. For me, music and dance still does it.

Ruthie was a prostitute, who lived on the third floor. She loved us kids and used to make big brown shopping bags full of popcorn for all of our parties. She believed kids should have fun because once you grew up it was "another story." She was quite a character and a fun person. Needless to say, my dad wanted me to have nothing to do with her but she was a big woman with a big heart. Most of us kids were a little intrigued but knew we had to keep our distance, especially since she worked out of her apartment. When the Navy ships came into the shipyard, there were always a lot of sailors around. They came in over the roof and up the front stairway.

Ruthie liked me and told me I would be trouble when I got older. I was usually in trouble then, no matter how hard I tried to be good, so that didn't seem like a big leap. When the men weren't there she taught me how to soak clothes in starch, before you ironed them, to make them even better looking. The sailors had taught her, so she taught me. She also taught me to put my jeans under my mattress to make the crease really hard and then they would look great. It seemed to me at the time, that the sailors taught her as much as she taught them. I enjoyed going into Ruthie's apartment because it seemed so free and relaxed up there. She was very different from all the other women in the neighborhood. She had a funny laugh and she certainly laughed a lot when I was there.

It was much more normal in the projects to see that families were struggling to survive and, if the couple had no real connection between themselves, other than mutual responsibility, they were each alone in their own inner battle with failure, entrapment, anger, and despair. Throughout my life, I have seen it so often. If no one is being fed emotionally or spiritually, if there is no heart connection to another, depression and loneliness, even in the crowd, becomes a way of life. Living in a void, in emptiness, for some, becomes the accepted way of life that is eventually all that is expected and, sadly, it becomes all that is asked for. Even as I child, I could I see that way of being as occurring when people have let all their dreams die. Without dreams we lose our connection to our passion, to hope, to our life force, to all that makes us who we are. They reflect all that we are and all that we can become. I learned early that dreams are a necessity not a luxury.

For whatever reason, thankfully, there always seems to be those few, who in any environment, seem to be filled with a sense of life, with vibrancy, interest, curiosity, and hope. The Rose in Spanish Harlem speaks of this as do so many other stories or songs. For some reason, life seems to be open and alive for them, no matter where they are from or what they have lived. It is as if they are a part of their world yet not. They are a part of their environment, yet they are also so much more than it. That, to me, is intriguing and a gift, a gift I believe I had after I began to dream. For me, I was very much a part of my world yet I never felt as if I really belonged and I never really wanted to stay. It would take me a lot of years before I could understand all the conflicting feelings and emotions that resulted from that.

One of the ways in which I did belong was in my attachment to my neighbors. They all seemed to have so much pain. Even as a young child, I could see it, and feel it, yet I rarely knew how to alleviate it. As an adult, that sensing ability became one of the greatest gifts I could share with my clients in helping them articulate their pain in order to alleviate it. We had a woman on the first floor who was also a prostitute, like Ruthie, but she was hardly ever home. Her two children and her husband were usually there, however. He often asked me to babysit while he went out. I got a chance to do my homework, eat a whole bag of potato chips, and have a Coke all to myself. It was a great job. Rather than pay me with cash, he would give me "hot" clothing or take me for Chinese food, a real treat in those days. The children became so attached to me that they would often follow me to school and I would have to leave the school yard with one on a hip and the other in tow to take them back home before school started. Again, I got in trouble.

I was becoming the mother and caretaker in the neighborhood, very early in my life. On my way to school I would often give peanut butter and crackers to the drunks asleep in the gutter. My dad would be angry that the food was disappearing so fast and now, with some humor, I can see that as a rather cruel thing to do when I realize how dry their mouths must have been already, But what does a young child know? This was all temporary. I knew I wanted to live life and dreamed of becoming a Rockette someday. I wanted all the glamour and high life I imagined they had in New York City. Although my mom told me I was too lazy to be a Rockette, I wanted to hold onto that dream for a long time and I did. It allowed me to believe that all this would pass. I would get out. When we need and want hope, we find it and oftentimes in a dream. How many times has someone told you that your dreams weren't "realistic," or that you didn't have what it takes? Did you give your power away or did you hold tighter and claim your dreams as yours? No one can take your dreams away unless you give them up.

I really was a good kid, just precocious. I could jump fences better than any boy in my neighborhood and with years of playing chicken (racing on our bikes toward one another to see who turned away first), I only got one permanent scar. When I felt ready for bigger stuff, I tried to explore a life of crime as well. It seemed wild, daring and so alive. In being honest, have you ever thought that "crime" was an exciting outlet? Although it seemed like there was never a chance to be really bad. There was one time when I thought I could put something over on everyone and really hit the big time and start a wild life without anyone seeing me. If this worked, I could see myself in a leather jacket, on a Harley Davidson, with a real man in front of me (at least one old enough to drive) flying across the country as free as a bird.

Although it has been over 40 years, I can still remember it, and feel it all, as if it was yesterday. I was about 9 and I saw a $.25 watch at the Five & Dime. I had never stolen a thing in my life and I was walking the line between being a good kid or "trouble" as they called those other kids. It was a totally spur of the moment thing on a Saturday morning but it was like I was getting my big break to go wild. I was ready. I slowly put this watch, (I thought with great finesse) into my pocket and so casually walked to the door. As soon as I got my first foot outside, the church across the street starting striking 12 times for the noon bell. I thought I would die on the spot, stabbed in the heart, twisting in the wind. God let me know in that instant, He never misses a thing and if I ever thought I could put something over on Him, I was insane. The whole walk home I waited for lightening to strike me dead. I had put the watch back so fast no one could have known I took it, but I just knew I had really done it this time for God to have to intercede.

I was dead meat. I was convinced my parents, mother superior, the principal, and everyone else in authority knew. As hysterical as it is now when I look back, I can assure you, it has never in my life ever again crossed my mind to steal anything from anybody under any circumstances. There are some lessons you just don't ever forget. Even when you change your perspective, the physical memory remains. As my girlfriend Theresa, another ex-nun, says, "once a Catholic, always a Catholic." There are some things locked on a cellular level. Fear, guilt, and trepidation are some of those things. Thank God for humor. It helps compensate. I have told my patients often, "Sanity doesn't mean you have it all figured out. It just means you know where your craziness is so it can't control you anymore." When they try to tell me I am the only one they have ever met who has it all together, I agree with them that I have it all together, it's in a pile in the closet.

To this day I do not believe in coincidences. I believe that what many see as coincidences are actually messages and that they serve a purpose. I see "coincidences" as God's way of letting us know something special was meant to happen and did. If we choose to be conscious in our living, we can see "coincidences" happening all the time. To me they are the Holy Spirit's way of reminding us that s/he is around, that we are not alone. They are messages that can remind us that we are always living on so many levels simultaneously. Most importantly, they are also our way of remembering that this is a spiritual journey we are walking. Nothing is without meaning.

# Chapter Two
## Adolescence

*Our dreams change as we change, grow as we grow,*
*and become more defined as we become more defined.*

I HAD BEEN IN PUBLIC SCHOOL THROUGH the fifth grade and had excelled academically all along. I was a good girl who got almost all A's on my report card and worked hard, so I got to do special errands for my teachers. I remember taking envelopes from one elementary school to another every week during class hours. The teachers trusted me and it felt so life giving to be treated with respect. I wonder how many teachers know how powerful their treatment of children can be in transforming their lives and their self-image. School for so many is the only nurturing, and safe, place they know. It is a gold mine for growth if it is used that way. I felt freer, less afraid, less overwhelmed there. There was a clear consistency. If you did this, this happened; if you did that, that happened. I loved it. It didn't change every day or a few times a day depending upon your parent's mood. You didn't get punished or beaten for not knowing exactly how they felt about something at any given moment. When children grow up with a time bomb like we did, what they need more than anything is constancy and predictability. Outside of school, I could get into trouble without even knowing it, but in school life was good and I excelled. All that changed when my parents decided, at puberty, to send me to Catholic school.

My parents had decided that the Catholic school would be good for me and the younger ones as well. You got a great education, and the nuns watched over you. As so many girls do, when they don't get the gentle nurturance and care they need at home, I had decided boyfriends were the way to go. They made me feel special, loved, and appreciated. In those days, though, a kiss on the lips was enough to send anyone to confession on Saturday night (or have your little sister pray for you) so it was all pretty chaste. From my first "friendship" ring in the first grade to the high school dances on Friday nights, I had always had a boyfriend. If I broke up with one on Saturday morning, I was "going steady" with someone else by Saturday night. True love and/or male friendship got confused more than once at that age. Unfortunately, I see so many people who still get those two confused at this point in their lives. Male and female friendship is not something we were ever taught a great deal about. That needs to change.

In any event, as a result of all this and more, I was sent off to Catholic school in the 6th grade so the nuns could keep an eye on me. It also guaranteed that I could get into the all-girl Catholic high school, which was very important since my parents didn't trust the public high school, which was co-ed. Little was it known that every parent in the area who feared puberty was sending their daughters to the nuns. Some had good reason, if I do say so myself, but… The end result was that every wild, and potentially wild, girl in the radius of St. Augustine's Parish was now in my class. I don't think that was at all what my parents had in mind. It was a comedy of errors. If humor wasn't developed before this, it was going to be very soon. That poor 6th grade Sister, God bless her and save her; she needed it and so did we. During our recess time, I learned all those things good girls in the public school never learned. During class time, I learned so much more.

The Catholic school was 2 years ahead of the public school academically so all of us who transferred in were way behind the group who had come up through the ranks. For the first time, I was not really smart or ahead of the class. For the first time, I didn't have all the answers. I didn't like it at all. We spent a lot of time after school studying and trying to catch up. That was the year I realized my parents didn't really credit me with brains, God gave me them, but they did blame me for my behavior, or personality. The good stuff was God's, the bad stuff was mine. Consequently, bonding with the other girls became extremely important. We all knew we were sent there to be watched over. That connection made it natural for adolescent girls to begin passing notes and giggling a great deal. Sister would imitate our giggling but not like those notes at all. My life of "crime" finally began. About once every few weeks, Sister would ask to see my parents at the convent after dinner to discuss my behavior. Usually it was about passing notes, and no matter what code we developed the nuns always figured them out. I had visions of them, after dinner, sitting around solving the code of the day. The notes were usually about boys. In as much as I feared all those evenings, I actually grew to respect the Sister I had. She honestly loved us and wanted us to grow up and get out of there. I once asked her why she picked on me so much and she said, "Dorothy, you only pick apples from a tree that bears good fruit. You are worth it." To this day I could cry when I think of this little nun saying that to me. I always seemed to have someone in my life who believed in me. What a gift that was and so needed.

Something happened to me that year. I think it came from the realization that someone could actually care for me enough to put all that extra time in. Even with all those evening visits and the detentions I got (sitting for one hour in a locked room with the lights off and all the shades drawn with some strange Sister up front listening to all of us breathing), I really felt the faith she had in me. Because of her, I realized how much more of me there was than I had ever seen before. I started to feel a solidity I never knew I possessed. I couldn't show it on the outside but I had begun to have hope, to believe that there was more to my life than I had been aware of, that there was more to me than I had been aware of. I didn't act on it, but I also didn't forget it. I would come back to it years later. Someone had seen me, had really, really seen me and in doing so, had allowed me to experience me in a way I had never known possible. She was one of the many gifts I would be given along the way. She was one of the angels, in physical form, that walk the earth with us all the time. Some are visible, some are not. Angels are real, very, very real. Think back on your own journey. How many have walked beside you through the years?

When I started high school, I had all the excitement of any girl about to become a woman but not knowing when or how. My home life was such that I was developing an ulcer; since the 4<sup>th</sup> grade it had been an issue, but now things were getting worse. I was taken to a doctor and treated for "acute anxiety." The situation between my parents was worse each year and with 2, almost 3, teenagers in a small apartment it was way too much for them to handle. My mother's desire to get out of South Boston and my dad's desire for the wife and family of his dreams were moving further and further out of reach and each felt it. When I most needed assurance and comfort, I was the one who needed to be strong. A pattern had developed in my life that would last for decades. I took over the tendency to put my needs or wants aside so that I could help others; however, at some point, I could not even identify what my personal needs were any longer. My "need" was to love, support, and protect others. I took it as a given life task. School again became my safety net. It was there that I would be safe, and, I knew all my brothers and sisters were in their classes and safe as well. At 13, I started working after school to help pay for my uniform and to have some spending money. I had been baby-sitting for years but now I was working in a hospital as a dietary aid in the kitchen and delivering meals to the patients. The goal for many of us was to turn 16 so we could work on a cash register and make "real money" in a grown-up job at Filene's or Jordan Marsh, two of the big department stores in Boston.

Working made all my friends and classmates feel freer and more grown-up than anything else. The major obstacle, for many of us, in getting to work, believe it or not, was French. In our junior year of high school, we had this little Irish nun who tried to teach us how to speak French. Talk about the blind leading the blind… None of us knew French but we sure as all heck knew enough to know it didn't sound like this. We were told laughing was not allowed. But let me tell you. YOU try not laughing at this scene. You have a group of adolescent girls sounding like they come from the projects, with an Irish nun, all trying to speak French. The tower of Babel had nothing on us. LaBiblioteque became a word that caused more laughter than any other word ever did. If we got detention, which was not uncommon, we had to do it right after school and that meant being late for work. Repression became a way of life. Nonetheless, we were in stitches most of that hour. Poor Sister, she was such a good soul but discipline in French class was more than anyone could ask for. Consequently, I, along with many others, failed most of our tests. Make-up tests were also after school. It seemed as if we were destined to be stuck there while work, and our lives, waited outside. Whatever stress I left at home, I picked up in French class. This one, however, usually had a lot of laughter right under it.

Every September when classes started again, we always watched to see who returned. The Sisters would not allow pregnant girls in school. So anyone who got pregnant over the summer or who started to show over the summer couldn't return. It was always a process of elimination. A few dropped off for prostitution but the rest were pretty much all pregnant. I always started the class by saying, thank you God, it wasn't me. My father had threatened to kill me if that ever happened. So you can rest assured, I took his words seriously and never ever risked that one. If Satan didn't get me, my father would. It was definitely a no-win situation. I would like to claim my virginity as a show of good virtue. But in truth, it was a show of sheer terror. I always wished I had the nerve of those that tried and didn't get caught, but it never came and I never went looking for too long.

By my junior year, we also started studying American History. We had a new girl in our class who had moved in from "down south." (In truth, pretty much everything was south of us). When it came to discussing civil rights and Martin Luther King, she and I were definitely on opposite sides of the fence. Our wonderful teacher realized it very soon in the year and did me one of the greatest favors of my high school years. She decided that Diane and I should each prepare for a debate presenting opposite sides of the story. The class would then see who could present the best arguments. My 6th grade nun had shown me that I possessed something of value and this nun was giving me permission, and even encouragement, to show it. I had tried to never really stick out before. I tried to blend in, it was safer that way and safety meant a lot to me growing up. She taught me to begin taking risks, to speak my mind on an issue even if someone disagreed completely. If I believed my point of view, she believed I should be able and willing to defend it. From a home where I was never allowed to disagree without getting a beating, this was a whole new concept that made me light headed, literally.

I could feel, in my body, the transformation that was taking place. I began to walk taller, to feel differently about myself and about life. I began to come alive and get excited about school and about me. I began to see that so much is possible. That there was a whole world out there waiting if I wanted to join in. It was as if someone had just opened up the doors and the windows and let life and the world in. I wanted to fly and all she did was ask me to head up a debate showing the rightness of Martin Luther King and all he believed in. I couldn't believe it. I counted, I mattered, and I had something to offer and in return the whole world was opening up. All of our lives we are preparing for the future while we live in the present. How all of this was going to play into my future is an amazing adventure.... I no longer needed the dream of the Rockettes. I moved beyond it. I didn't believe I was too lazy but I did come to believe that I could make a different kind of life for myself. I had found me and figured I could make a free, joy-filled life if I just had the chance.

Around this time, my girlfriends had told me about a boy I just had to meet. He was a member of another parish, a Polish church I had never been to, St. Mary's. The downstairs at this church had a teen center where the kids could hang out under some level of supervision. I went the next afternoon with my girlfriends to meet this boy who in truth was much more of a man since all the boys I knew were in my grade. He had previously been a member of this teen center but was now in the Army and had recently turned 20. In those days, four years was a world of difference. Nonetheless, we spent the next two days together before he was sent to Panama. We agreed to write daily and date again when he came home on leave. Little did I know what changes that would bring to my life. Perhaps because he was older, or perhaps because I was coming into my own, or perhaps for both reasons, writing every day, and the safety it provided permitted each of us to explore as much of ourselves in writing as we explored of each other. We came to share everything with one another, our dreams, our fears, and our lives as we wanted them to be.

I had never kept a diary. Writing to him, caused me to listen to my own words, it supported me in reaching out of the box, in allowing myself to dream even further. In my innocence, I saw him as being very sophisticated, mature, and worldly. He in truth was seeing other parts of the world; he was having experiences I didn't think I would ever have. I was frightened of his worldliness and yet attracted to his gentleness and understanding. I had never been far from South Boston and didn't know that I ever would be. As a result, I took risks and shared with him dreams I never would have shared with others. Somehow I thought he would understand. He was older and yet had spent his high school years in the seminary so he was equally innocent and unaware of the grand world around him. He came to see me as being older, his equal. We fell in love over time.

After spending his first leave together, meeting his parents and his brother, and talking endlessly, Ray went back to Panama. I was so excited at the reality of knowing so much about him in person and at what we had created through these letters and the Sunday afternoon phone calls that he made to a phone booth near my home, that I believed the dreams we had spoken of could come true. I saw so much more for me than Southie and so much more for him. We both had dreams bigger than where we were. My parents approved of him yet were not happy with the age difference. I now suspect they thought this would fade before he returned again so they let it go on. One day, however, he sent me pictures of three hope-chests that were hand-carved by the Indians of Panama. He wanted me to pick one so that he could send it to me. We talked of getting married when I graduated from high school.

My mother found those pictures and immediately ended our relationship. I could no longer write to him or get his letters. His weekly Sunday afternoon phone calls were not permitted and it felt as if my life was over. This argument went on for weeks although the feelings went on much longer. It didn't make sense. There was a huge vacuum in my life and we couldn't even talk about it. This man who had called me to become more of me, who encouraged me to dream, who wanted to marry me, was gone. I knew life with him would be different and I wanted that and him, yet that life was something we never got to explore or develop. Amazingly, a psychic reader has recently told me that Ray was meant to leave a powerful bookmark at that point in my life, to be continued later when we were both ready.

In the midst of my pain and sadness, my father believed that I simply needed a new boyfriend, an Irish boy, who would never take me away from Southie where I belonged. My mother wanted me to put everything behind me and focus on school. I just knew that I had a vacuum inside and couldn't explain it to Ray. I continued living my life, going to school, and working after hours. I met a boy my father approved of, who would stay in Southie. He was a wonderful guy. We spoke of marriage and the ten kids Ray and I had talked of. My thought was of getting married, and moving to a tenement and having an entire floor all to ourselves. It felt like the epitome of wealth. I was going to be filled with love for all of humanity. Michael was wonderful to look at, he treated me like a queen, his family loved me, and he had a good job as an electrician. What more could a good Irish girl from South Boston want? Especially a girl who could not speak to the man who taught her to dream big, and who knew her so well? Nothing I could put my finger on at the moment…. I thought Ray would hate me by now, thinking I had abandoned him, had left him for no reason. I imagined him with others and it hurt.

By senior year, I realized I wanted more. I had opened to dreams with Ray, to more options. I needed more than Southie now. I wanted to become a nurse or a social worker. I wanted to contribute. I wanted to have an impact and do something with my life. I did not want to be 25 with 6 children and 30 with a few more. I wanted something but I didn't know exactly what or how to get it any more. I asked my parents about college since I was in the college-prep program not the secretarial program. (Logic makes me wonder why the college-prep program?) As I said before, I was getting good grades but my folks never intended to send me to college so why did they have me take this??? No longer do I believe in coincidences. There is always a reason for everything even if we don't understand it ourselves, or, at the time. In any event, when I asked my dad about college, he said that he felt it was a waste of money to send girls to college. "They get pregnant and married (hopefully not in that order) and are a waste of money. I have boys to send to school. Boys need college." Why then had Ray been a threat to all this?

I tried to become a nurse but since our inner city schools were unaccredited, no nursing program I applied to would accept me. Not to be stopped, I decided that if I became a Catholic nun I would then be able to be a social worker and do what I wanted to do. I didn't understand that college was a part of the picture. I had never met a social worker. I just read about them and as a result I had no idea what their training was.

I knew some nuns were social workers. I just assumed it came with the clothing. I couldn't believe that I actually was thinking in terms of me as a real person who could create a life of her own. I was going to actually have a life, a career. I was going to have me. No words can describe what that means. I was going to exist, not in relationship to someone else but as me, as a woman. That was not something I had ever imagined. Even when I thought of being a Rockette, I thought of myself as my parent's daughter, just in a different place. Later, I thought of myself with Ray. With him gone, I could actually see myself as a separate human being. Someone who made life decisions on her own based on her own dreams and her visions. It was beyond words. The exalting freedom in that was beyond words. I had really grown up and made it out, alive and sane, and alone.

An additional reason for choosing religious life was even deeper than all that. Although I had been blessed with a number of good teachers, the few great ones happened to be nuns. There were two specifically who possessed something that I couldn't define at the time, but I wanted it. Later, I discovered it was called inner peace. Because they were the only two people I had ever met who possessed it, I figured the answer was in the convent. Combining that with wanting to help people who were stuck in poverty, without any idea of how to better themselves or get ahead, it was the perfect place to go. I wanted others to experience the freedom and breath of fresh air I had experienced when Sister asked me to debate. It was ironic that after all the detentions I had served, and all the trips my parents made to the convent after supper, I was to become a nun. I applied and became a Good Shepherd Sister. With all the communities that existed at that time, why that one was chosen is a story in itself. Let me share it.

Once I decided I wanted to enter the convent, I called a religious community in the area that did social work. I said I wanted to join and waited for them to be thrilled. . However, once they discovered that I was illegitimate, not one religious community in the United States would take me. My junior year teacher and the parish priest wrote to over 1,000 communities around the world to find one that would take an illegitimate child. They eventually found one in Canada that worked with prostitutes that was willing to risk allowing me inside as a member of their community.

No matter how hard our parents had tried to raise us correctly, Dad had adopted Bob and I and through the years mom and dad always took us to 9:00 mass on Sunday mornings. I remembered how we all had to starve from midnight until after receiving Holy Communion before we could have breakfast even on Christmas and Easter when we had all that candy just waiting to be eaten. I remembered how mom had washed all the clothes and I hung them out on the line, as soon as I could reach it, to make sure we were clean and ready for church. They gave us each a nickel for the collection box and made sure we genuflected before entering and leaving the pew in church. My parents spent years teaching us catechism, making sure we received all the sacraments and went to mass every first Friday. They raised a pack of good little Catholics and still I couldn't join religious life in the United States.

Yet these two people, a nun and a priest, were angels to me -- living breathing angels. They realized that some religious communities are under the Pope while others are under the supervision of the local bishop. One of them had found the community in Canada that had never had an illegitimate sister before but was willing to take a risk and let one in. I do not know if they thought I would corrupt all the "good" sisters or if they thought I would steal something. Stealing was definitely out of the picture. This was my dream. I was going to help people. I was going to find that inner peace that those other two nuns had and I was going to be a social worker. Nothing was going to stop me.

The community we found was called the Good Shepherd Sisters. Their formal name was The Sister Servants of the Immaculate Heart of Mary, SCIM. The Mother House was in Quebec, Canada. Wouldn't you know it? This was a French Canadian community and the older sisters only spoke French. I swear God has a terrific sense of humor. They would allow me to enter the community but I would be assigned to a foreign mission, in the United States. God bless these wonderful women. A large number of French Canadians had migrated south to Maine and Massachusetts in the USA, and so, many sisters were sent there to teach, nurse, and do social work. I would be assigned there, begin my training, and then work in that mission. Talk about finding a way around the system. God bless them. You have got to love women. They are creative little devils, aren't they?

# Chapter Three
## A Catholic Nun

*Dreams are meant to be lived for whatever the duration.*
*They are the gifts we give ourselves.*

GOING FROM THE PROJECTS TO THE CONVENT is an adventure I am thrilled I got to experience. I don't know if the shock was worse for the older Sisters or for me. We were truly from different worlds. In high school we tried to be sexy, by rolling our skirts up at the waist so that the bottom half of our knees showed. We didn't know about midriff bulge at the time so it wasn't a concern. Now I was going to wear an outfit that consisted of white cotton panties that came down to the knees, (they made boxers look racy), a cotton tee-shirt that came to my knees, black nylons (that were not really nylon since we mended them if they got holes), and a black slip with pockets that went to our knees. Over this we wore a huge black dress of serge (heavier than wool if you want my opinion), a collar with the crucifix hanging down, and long rosary beads hanging from the waist to just above the floor. To top it all off, we put a cotton bonnet on our heads and a huge coif over it which consisted of a bleach bottle formed in a half-circle with a black veil attached, which came below our waist in the back. Believe it or not, in the "habit," as it is called, I felt more beautiful, and more real, than I had ever felt before.

The ceremony we underwent on entrance day involved changing from our "lay" clothes into the habit of our community. It was a very sacred and special ceremony, symbolizing our giving up of one way of life and the beginning of another. There was certainly fear of letting go of the past, sadness at letting go of Michael, a very dear friend, since he had come with my family to take me to the convent, and some fear for the others I had left behind. With all this fear and apprehension, at the same time there was hope, anticipation, and wonder. I remember kneeling in awe at the sound of the Sisters' choir behind us, the ceremony the priest was conducting in front of us, and the realization that I was joining an organization that I knew nothing about. The only thing I was certain about, in every cell of my being, was that I belonged there. That was enough for me to surrender to whatever was to come. That inner knowing that this was where I belonged was as solid, as real, as any other sensation I had ever had. This was one I could identify with and accept fully.

Once I was a Good Shepherd Sister, I began a life that reached beyond anything I ever could have imagined. I never could have fathomed, on a conscious level, the peace, both inner and outer, that existed in religious life. There was no longer the violence or the screams in the night that had been a familiar part of my world until then. There was no despair as I had seen daily on the faces of so many people in South Boston. There was faith and Mother Superior saying that "God is in his heaven and all is right with the world." It was the fulfillment of a dream I had longed for. It fulfilled a child's dream to belong and have peace.

Initially, I was like a young child. Just tell me where to go and what to do and I will do it. As time went on and people started leaving, I became frightened that I was going to be asked to leave also. The old fears of being punished for something I knew nothing about kept coming up. There was a fear that I wasn't good enough and they would kick me out once they found out I had smoked or went to drive-ins with Michael or had tried a rum and Coke at a beach party, etc. As I started to feel at home, the fear was that I would lose it. Not being "good enough" was a theme in everything I did. It came from long before I entered the convent and would stay long after I left. Scars of our childhood don't necessarily heal easily. They need to be identified and then we need to have a lot of reinforcement in the opposite direction. For most of us, having self-worth comes after a long painful period of acknowledging our value and contributions, in spite of those inner messages. I was blessed in that all the Mother Superiors I had, enjoyed me and truly cared for me. They again were the angels I needed in my life at that time and they were preparing me for a future none of us ever could have anticipated.

Rather than being asked to leave at the end of the first year, as I had feared, I was able to go on with my class and become a novice after one year as a postulant. It was a glorious day where our willingness to follow our hearts and our faith, and to remain in religious life, was acknowledged in another ceremony. Sisters from all over came to celebrate and party with us. The initiation was over and now a more intense period of preparation for our vows was to take place. Later, having a younger group of new Sisters come in, made all of us feel like a mixture of the big sister and upper-class-man. It was validation that we had made it.

Life now consisted of getting up at 5:40 am and washing up in a bowl of water we had placed on our nightstands the night before. We slept in a huge room that was divided in aisles and "bedrooms" in such a way that it looked like hospital beds with curtains around them. It was like a huge hospital ward. In the morning, after we washed, we dressed. As novices, we now wore white veils that were similar in style to what the professed Sisters wore. After we dressed and made our beds, we opened the curtains around our individual areas and proceeded downstairs. We had prayers, meditation, and then Mass. After that, we got breakfast and then everyone headed off to do the housework chores they had been assigned for the year. When all that was done, we began our classes. I was finally getting to go to college, a surprise I never anticipated. Because the first two years of the novitiate are cloistered, we were not allowed to go onto campus, so the teachers came to us. Our Mistress of Studies, Sr. St. Robert, taught us many of the classes, but not all, so help from campus was called in. It was so much fun to be studying. After my junior year in high school, I really came to love learning and couldn't get enough. Sr. St. Robert said often, "Sisters, you don't need to know everything, you just need to know where to find it," and boy could Sr. St. Robert find everything. We all loved her. She was feisty. She kept all the rules but you knew, sometimes, she was walking on that thin line, real tight.

At lunch we took a break to eat and then went outdoors. We were allowed to talk for about a half-hour and usually played volleyball to let out a lot of "steam," as Mother would say. After our lunch break, we then went back to our studies until it was time for the Way of the Cross, more meditation, the rosary, and more prayers. After dinner we got to have community time and talk again before we went to our "rooms" to study.

Over the years, I have had so many people question me about "Why the convent?" "Why chastity?" "Why would a young girl do that?" It amazes me that with all that our lives entailed, with all the things that filled us, this is the one question that intrigues most people. None of us chose chastity. What we chose was a lifelong commitment to love, honor, and cherish all people and a deepening of our relationship with God. What we were choosing was a life filled with joyous service given in love. I have seen so many who chose service, but out of obligation, fear, or debt. Instead of doing good, they ended up with so much bitterness, anger, and resentment towards others. What a mistake! We were choosing in joy and so many of our needs were readily met, more so than for so many others. All our meals were cooked and provided. All our expenses were met. We always had a warm community to come home to and a Mother Superior who totally wanted what was best for us.

The life of a religious isn't about sacrifice of any kind. It is about growing in your ability to love yourself and all humanity and about deepening your understanding and relationship with God. As in any way of life, there are things that you give up. In having a child you sacrifice freedom, and take on an immense financial burden. In being married you sacrifice freedom to freely date whomever you please and you lose a lot of your own time and space. The point is what do you want to focus on? What is your priority? Is it worth it to you? I have not had one moment of regret. In truth, I have had years of gratitude for the gift those years were, even in the realization that I was not meant to stay there for life. For me, it was training ground, a haven from all the fears and pain, so that I could do what was needed before I could move on.

After one year as a postulant and one year as a novice, we were then ready to profess our vows of Poverty, Chastity, and Obedience to the community. We had completed preparation and were now ready to be considered active members of the community. In the Novitiate, all of the postulants and novices live apart from the professed Sisters. After profession, we moved to the other side of the house, with all the other professed Sisters. At that point, I became the "hairdresser" in our house. As a result, during our relaxed community times, I was often cutting someone's hair. It was a wonderful way to get to know someone better, especially if they spoke English. Also, after profession, life was a little less cloistered. We were professed so we were now able to attend classes on campus and prepare for our assignments. In our community, the "professional" sisters were nurses, teachers, or social workers. We also had sisters who cooked, did laundry, or handled all the other aspects of our lives. Although we had more freedom, silence was still a way of life. The silence was a gift we all loved. Some of us, however, found difficulty with it on occasion. As a novice I also worked hard to practice "custody of the eyes." That meant that instead of looking around as we walked, we looked down at the floor.

We also had "custody of the hands" which meant that we kept our hands locked in front of us, inside our very large sleeves. More than once, as I was walking down the corridor, I would come to the doors that separated the parlor area from the chapel and refectory. The doors were like they had in the old western saloons. (Tell me, why on earth would you put those in a convent?). In my overzealous desire to practice custody of the eyes, on occasion I didn't see the doors coming. WHAM! I would walk right into the door with my head. My coif would go flying. I would hold my head and burst into laughter, all during quiet time. If some Sisters were in chapel, they would come out to see what the noise was about. They would see me scurrying about trying to put my coif on and pretending nothing happened. Thankfully, one day, an older Sister was behind me and after she stopped her laughing, fearing she would embarrass me, she taught me a few tricks of the trade. You don't look straight down; you look at an angle. It sure did help me a lot in a number of different situations. It is amazing the things we don't tell people because we assume they will know. Don't assume much, it is usually a mistake. It can take so little to help someone out.

So many things struck me funny in there. As I said before, I was blessed with having Mother Superiors who loved me. They could see that I was slightly different from your typical nun, whatever that means, but that my heart was in the right place and that nobody was more committed than I was. As a result, for the first time in my life, I felt absolutely loved, unconditionally. They affirmed me every chance they could and they encouraged me to keep trying new things, and to reach out more, to dream more, and plan more. They began taking away the fears that said I couldn't or I shouldn't and said "Sister go for it." In psychotherapy terms, they were "re-parenting" me and in a way I never knew existed.

Ironically, in as much as they affirmed me to reach out and to follow my heart, it was in doing just those things that I realized I didn't belong. When I lived in Maine, after profession of vows, there were two drivers, for over 65 nuns. I was one of the drivers. I had been asked to teach high school boys CCD, religious classes, on Sunday nights. A 15 year old male student would pick me up so that I didn't have to take the only car in case someone needed it in an emergency. One of the older Sisters began to fear that I might be threatening my vows (Poverty, Chastity and Obedience) by riding with him and so Mother suggested that I take an older Sister with me. Now this sophomore in high school was much younger than I and needed me as a confidante and as a mother figure more than he needed me as a girlfriend. If I were going to be tempted, it would have been with the gorgeous visiting priest not with a young boy. For the first time ever, I risked speaking my truth when it contradicted Mother's and said that if I needed to take a chaperone I would not teach. I would not be humiliated and treated like a child. I was a grown woman and if I didn't want to keep my vows, I never would have taken them. Thankfully, Mother had faith in me and I continued teaching without supervision and she spoke to the concerned older Sister. What had happened, however, was that I began to see that my vows and my life would always be under the scrutiny of everyone I lived with and they all got to have a say. I was becoming much more independent than I had ever realized.

Campus was an amazing adventure that also brought my independence to light, even more. We went to an all-male college. It was all-male except, of course, for some nuns. Makes you wonder, doesn't it? Here we were perfectly healthy women, attending college and being seen as neutered, at least by the administration. This was my first post-high school experience with men and it was as mixed as any of my experiences of the next few decades would be. It began with college boys asking some others, and myself, if we wanted to take a walk in the woods so they could show us nature. (We lived in the convent; we weren't born there.) I also met so many of these boy/men needing a mother and turning to me for support in school studies, in loneliness at being away from home for the first time, and for help with sexual identity. We had jumped right into the frying pan as they say. By the end of that period, we also had drugs moving onto campus, girls where allowed in, and, race and Vietnam were becoming hot issues. We had been so sheltered and quickly we were considered qualified to help, support, and encourage.

One evening, I got called by some of the new girls on campus because a friend had taken drugs and was sitting on the goal post talking to angels. When I mentioned to Mother that I needed the car immediately to go to campus which was about 15 minutes away, she reminded me that the laity would be scandalized seeing a nun out alone, late at night. The worst part she said was that I was going to a mostly male college with 80 girls and 500 males at this point. As a result, I was not allowed out. The girls had no one to turn to, and realized they needn't ever call me again at night whatever the need because I couldn't come. After several incidents like this one, on top of the others, I started to have an uneasy feeling. With all the difficulties I ran into, they were never about my feeling limited by my vows or my commitment to service in community, they were always about the fears others had about such things. And about the "image" good nuns were supposed to portray. I still loved the atmosphere of silence, the community, and the shared dreams, but I was feeling so confused by the expectations of others. It was almost as if we needed to choose whether to be good Christians or good nuns and yet that is such an insane concept. How and why would they put us in this dilemma? It made no sense to me.

After, I had finished my college years, at least for that moment, and was at my next assignment, I discovered nothing was going to change. One of the last incidents I had was really totally innocent. I had been stationed at a residential treatment center. I was assistant housemother for a group of girls from 6–16. They had come to us from Reform School, the Youth Service Board, the House of Correction, and Solitary Confinement. They had suffered so much already and we were to do treatment for a minimum of two years in conjunction with a staff of psychologists, state social workers, and a psychiatrist. Needless to say, some days the work was very heavy and overwhelming. One day about 5 of us from my Novitiate class and the class above us all decided, on a whim, to take the kids' bicycles and pedal down the road to another house our community had. We had friends stationed there who were teachers and they had the day off. Well, we tied our dresses up, (yet still well below our knees) the way we usually did, and took off. Here was a line of nuns going down the road, next to traffic, veils flying, to visit their friends. Well…

When we got to their house 10-15 minute away, one of the Sisters, quietly called our Mother General who lived at the mother house in Quebec, Canada, who in turn called Mother Provincial who lived in Saco, Maine who then called our Mother Superior at our house in Methuen, Massachusetts. By the time we got home, from a 20-minute visit in Lawrence, we were informed of the international incident we had caused. There was a fear of scandalizing the laity, (who were probably in stitches telling this story to everyone they knew since they had all honked their horns and waved as they drove by), disobeying proper etiquette for nuns, and leaving our property without permission. Here we were, a group of college educated women in our 20's, out for a ride to let off steam and to feel free after so long. We were just "getting away from it all" in such an innocent fashion and yet we were creating an international incident. It became clear that this was not working. The guidelines defined by priests, who knew nothing of our life, governed every facet of it. We wanted freedom to live our lives as needed, to recondition the laity, and to perform our tasks as they were required, not according to some guidelines set by others who do not even know what they entail.

Shortly after all of this, I was permitted to take my first week-long "vacation" out of community, a permission which was granted after a number of years. I went back to my parents' home. From there, I visited girlfriends, saw the old neighborhood, went to old restaurants, and was also taken by my dad to visit Ray's parents in their new home. They had loved me as their own and the two fathers had somehow become friends over the years, perhaps commiserating over their loss. It was an exciting, scary, and odd experience with a wide mixture of emotions. As I sat there in their living room, in my religious habit, with a cup of tea in my lap, unknown to me, Ray's mom went into the kitchen and called Ray to come for dinner.

Shortly after, he showed up with his wife of one year, and their newborn daughter. The shock for Ray and I was obvious and yet we responded differently. Within minutes I told my dad it was time to leave. It seemed appropriate since all of a sudden I felt very much out of place. I didn't belong there although my picture was still on their mantle and was to remain there for years to come. The look on Ray's face was of shock yet I, in my fear, embarrassment, and shock, I saw anger instead. Perhaps I had been expecting that for years and saw it whether it was there or not. Whatever he felt, it was clear that neither of us knew how to respond so my leaving their home feeling very much the outsider was the least awkward thing I could do for both of us. I couldn't accept he had a wife and a daughter, the daughter I was supposed to have.

After returning home to religious life, and in quick succession, a couple more "incidents," Mother Superior and I talked long and hard about all my feelings. She was very open to having me go to another community that may be less restrictive but it was clear to me that I loved this community. If I were going to stay in religious life, it would be here. It wasn't so much the particular community; it was the fact I no longer felt that I belonged there and the fact that priests who were not in religious life defined us. As I mentioned before, the local bishops or the Pope generally govern religious orders. It was they who decided what we needed to do or not do and what we could do or couldn't do. Even in leaving religious life, I needed to have our local bishop dispense me from my vows (the equivalent of an annulment). He was not a member of our community or of our world. He was a nice guy but he wasn't one of us and yet his power was enormous. Having lived without magazines, television, or radio for all those years, I had somehow, nonetheless, become what they called a feminist, through no intention of my own. I had been educated, taught to love unconditionally, to serve the Christian community and the world, as a competent professional, and yet I was still expected to be submissive to someone else's view of appropriate behavior, someone who had more freedom than I ever would achieve inside, and yet who invalidated my need for that same freedom. It seemed at this point, that the system had begun working against itself.

They had supported me in becoming this strong and confident woman and yet needed me to surrender my sense of justice and fairness. The growth I had been led there to develop had been achieved. I had been loved like never before and trained, educated, and blessed beyond words. They had shown me a side of me, and a side of life, I had never known. They had opened up the world much more clearly and the awareness that we are living our lives on so many levels simultaneously. I had achieved things I never would have achieved if I hadn't entered religious life. I went to college; I became a social worker; and I had years where I could focus solely on my own personal growth and self-definition. I had found me and I did it in an environment where I was loved, safe, and cherished. Many of the older Sisters came to recognize my sincerity and my innate goodness even though they had initially been frightened of me. Although initially we didn't speak much, when we did, I spoke with the language of the projects. It was all I knew. One actually told me years later, that some had expected me to pull a knife from my pocket if I ever got really mad. They came instead to see innocence and a joy in living that brought laughter and childlike faith to the houses I lived in. Some actually wondered what trouble I would get into next. They enjoyed waiting and watching. They knew it would be innocent and usually hysterical to watch. It was like a comedy of errors. It was our own little slapstick humor but with no malice at all. None, however, ever expected it to lead to my leaving community. One wonderful, innocent, Sister said to me once, "Sister, if you could just hold all your opinions for about 15 years, the Sisters will all catch up with you. You will be the leader of our community someday. You were born to be the leader." God bless her. If I had to hold my opinions for 15 years, I would be dead and they would lose their leader anyway. I loved her for her faith in me, but realized, again, I couldn't do this, for too many reasons to mention.

For many of us, it takes a great amount of faith, trust, and courage to follow what we know in our heart is right. In listening to our inner knowing, we go on even if we don't know what lies ahead. I just knew that somehow, and trusted that in time, everything would all work out. It always does. I just knew this place was no longer right for me. In knowing that, I learned that sometimes a dream is just meant to take us to the next step, to the next part of our journey. As a child, I had had a dream that changed before I had a chance to live it. Now I had a dream that transformed my life into so much more than it ever could have been. Dreams are meant to change and grow as we change and grow. Initially that was a frightening thought. We had been taught that you reach a level early and then just coast through the rest of your life. Now, it meant that life was always in transition. After the fear around that left, what a wonderful discovery that was. Life was free and ever changing, consciously or otherwise.

Wonderfully and ironically, it was while I was in religious life that my spiritual life took off. As dogmatic as it could be, it also left room for the personal, intimate development of a relationship with God. Inside I learned the massive difference between religion and spirituality. Since then, religion, the following of a doctrine, has lost all importance to me. My spirituality, my relationship with all those in the Spirit world, God, the Angels, and others, has become the most significant part of my inner life. It has continued to grow and change along with my relationship with the Holy Spirit, my guides, and my inner knowing. Finally, after 5 years, I left that part of my life, that dream, with more than I ever could have asked for. I was so aware, that I was being led, and had always been, as well as leading. The term co-creator had become so obvious to me. We are given all the opportunities we need, to get where we need to go and to grow. It is our responsibility, our option, and our freedom to choose to take them or not.

At this point in my life, when I hear people say to me, "I have no option," I look to see what opportunities they are refusing to acknowledge. We always have so many. In what way are they choosing to play victim? Victim is a position of choice. If you are in a situation you hate, or fear, why do you choose to remain? Oftentimes I would hear from patients, "I have nowhere else to go." I would say, "That is what you allowed yourself to believe before you came into this room. Now let me list several options." Inevitably, I would hear excuses as to why every one of those options was "impossible." What some were was difficult or unpleasant, but not impossible. Linda Ronstadt has a song out which I love. In it she sings: "The impossible just takes a little time." Ain't that the truth! When you feel stuck, look at why. What freedoms are you too frightened to consider? A move, because you don't know anyone? A breakup, because you are frightened of being alone? A relationship, because you may be hurt? A commitment, because it may not be the right choice? An ultimatum, because you may not like the answer?

As far as leaving religious life, my family members each had their own opinion. My brother Bob had said upon entering that no sister of his would ever join an organization like this and as a result I was no longer his sister. He never once came to visit me in all the years I was in. I didn't see him until the year before I left when he came, not to see me, but to tell me that my parents were getting a divorce. My mother had asked him to testify and he wanted to know what I thought and that I supported him. I know he needed to know he wasn't alone and that I still treasured him and had accepted his fear and anger over losing me even though I didn't let them control my decision to enter. This visit was not an acceptance of my choice only a reaffirmation that we were still in this together. It was a compromise. I loved it. My eventual leaving was to be the official reconnection as family for us.

My dad refused to talk to me when I entered religious life. He couldn't handle losing his little girl and he certainly didn't like losing control over my life. He wanted 20 grandchildren and I was supposed to give them to him. He would come to visit me each month but talk to my sister Mary. (We were allowed to visit family for one hour each month. They would all drive for 3 hours, visit for one hour, and then drive three hours back,) He would say, "Mary, Mike has enough money to buy Dottie a diamond if she comes out."

or "Mary, a friend of mine, a car dealer, will give Dottie her own car if she leaves this place." Nonetheless, one Sunday, while I was in the Novitiate, avoiding me, he brought in the grinders I loved for all those in the novitiate with me. He wanted us to have a special treat. His generosity got the better of him. He also knew I could not be manipulated anymore. My mother believed that with one of us in religious life, all of us, including her, would get into heaven. Somehow that was a deal God made with parents who gave a child back. God bless her soul, my mother spent her life making up for sins she never committed. Needless to say, when I left, Dad was thrilled. He had his daughter back. My mother had come to accept my choice as being mine to make.

Mary used to bring Michael up. He wanted to see that I was OK. When he finally believed I would never leave, he came to tell me about a girl he had met and thought he would marry as long as he knew for a fact that I would never leave. If there was a chance, he would wait for as long as it took. I had been blessed to be loved by two men who were so different from my Dad. One offered me a world and taught me to risk, love, and to dream, another gave me confidence and kindness when I needed it most. I do believe there was a reason I never thought of leaving until Mike got engaged. We each had different journeys to travel and had given the other exactly what was needed for the time we were together. He was another angel in my life when I needed him so much. Mike showed me a man's ability to love another without rage but with definite boundaries. I will always respect him and be grateful he came into my life.

From all that I had been through, and all that I had learned about me, about life and about relationships, I knew in my soul that things would always turn out OK. If I trusted my inner knowing, if I trusted my own inner sense, I would end up exactly where I needed to be. As a result, I have developed a pattern. No matter what I am considering, I always take a moment to look at the worst possible consequence of this choice as well as the worst possible consequence of not making this choice. After I consciously began taking risks, risks that took me to greater freedom and greater self-expression, I began to realize that I ALWAYS land on my feet. I began to trust my judgment, my inner knowing, and my innate awareness that I knew what was right for me more than anyone else in the world. With that, I began to be really and truly free. Think about it. Who do you admire and envy more, the person who is sweet and yet governed (and limited) by fear or the person who is fully alive and has jumped into life with both feet ready to live it completely? A Japanese proverb says it is best to honor the man who has had many failings because he is the man who has tried much. He may have failed, but he got up and tried something else. Life goes on and, without fear being in charge, it is a real adventure and rarely do we know where it will lead.

# Chapter Four
## Transition

*Sometimes we need to find ourselves*
*before we can find a dream.*

WHEN I LEFT RELIGIOUS LIFE, I HAD no idea where I was going next in terms of geographic area, profession, or anything else. I just knew I needed to leave. I began by taking the two months necessary to get dispensed from my vows. I may have been leaving but I still honored that way of life for those for whom it worked, those who belonged there. To show my respect, I chose to follow the routine that had been established. The Sisters gave me a wonderful, although bittersweet, send off. They had a party for me and gave me boxes of toothpaste, toothbrushes, and soaps, etc. They even gave me money to buy lay clothes and what an event that was…When I entered, we thought it was wild to show the bottom of our knees; now they were wearing micro-minis and hot pants. Oh God!!! How on earth was I ever going to fit in?

There was an association called Bearings. It was a support organization that helped ex-priests and ex-nuns get their bearings in adjusting to the lay world and boy did we need help. Life changes so much and so fast in such a short period of time. At the same time that I left religious life, guys were coming home from Vietnam and talking about cultural shock. Although our experiences were radically different, I certainly understood what they were talking about. I looked up one old girlfriend and had lunch to catch up. She proceeded to tell me I needed to get on birth control pills that afternoon. To say I was shocked is an understatement. When I asked why on earth I would do that (they weren't even on the market when I entered), she told me I may meet someone special today or I may get raped, since that happened "all the time" now. Rather than helping me adjust to being out, this lunch filled me with acute anxiety. I now understood why so many women were on Valium. What an insane place the world had become. I did not go on the pill at that time, or take Valium, but I sure did look around me a lot more than normal for a while. Actually, she then went on and had a "coming out" party for me at a bar in Cambridge. When I went into the convent, I was just out of high school and so I had never been in a real bar. Now there was a coming out of the convent party in one. Not much made sense and I felt as if I was spinning a lot. Carol had a cake made that said, "LOOK OUT WORLD, DOTTIE'S BACK." I may have been "wild" and fun loving in high school but this was a whole new league and I was in way over my head. She told me I needed to learn to drink Harvey Wall Bangers with grenadine since that was the drink of the day. Well, one drink later, I vomited the whole ride home. My entry back into the lay world was not a very pretty sight. I had no idea about creating a dream for my future; I couldn't even figure out where I had landed.

Thankfully, the people at Bearings decided to get me a place to stay with another ex-nun who would temporarily put me up until I got a job and got settled on my own. She was like a big sister. That poor thing had no idea what hit her and neither did I. She was a very quiet, reserved thing with very particular ways. I, on the other hand, had one suitcase of clothes, hadn't washed a thing in years, since the Sisters in laundry handled all that, and had not held money in a very long time.

It is the details of adjustment that are the killers, partly because no one anticipates they will be your downfall. They try to protect you in the major decisions but it is the little ones that you are dealing with all day and all night. Here are a few examples: I went to the store to buy something and, with a long line behind me, the clerk gave me bills in all amounts as change. I tried to put them all in order with the lowest in front and then moving back in progression with singles and then fives, tens, and twenties. Being a Friday night, with a long line waiting and rushing, I did not make any friends on that trip to the store. Also, I was no longer wearing all those layers of clothes and so I was always cold. Carol had told me that fake furs were in and very warm so I should buy one. She had also dyed her hair blond and I loved it so she told me I should buy a wig first and see if I liked it. If you can imagine, one week since I was in the habit, and I was now wearing a leopard skin fake fur coat and a blond wig. As I said, I was in WAY over my head AND there was no going back. What could I do but go forward????

While all these adjustments were going on, Bearings got me a job as an assistant to the secretary of the dean in the business school at Boston College. Their thoughts were that I would have a job in the lay world but still be surrounded by Jesuits (that was supposed to be a good thing) so that it wouldn't be an all-at-once adjustment. I was living with this poor little thing who had no idea how to guide me since she had no idea where on earth I was coming from and I was blowing her well ordered life while walking around in a blond wig and a leopard skin coat. Now I think it was hysterical but then I was close to hysterics. It was all too much. I had dropped onto a foreign planet and had no idea how to phone home. My position of assistant to the secretary of the dean was to be short-lived, as you can imagine.

When I wasn't working, I looked up other old friends from high school. Some were on welfare and raising their kids alone, some were struggling to get ahead, and some had died in prison or Vietnam. My older brother Bob had left home and gone as far away as possible. It was a pattern in our family. He was teaching at the

American College in Zambia, Africa. My sister Mary was living in Barcelona, Spain and had a leather goods shop with her first husband who was Catalonian. My brother Joe was living on a Kibbutz in Israel. Jim, the youngest, was starting to work for the airlines at Logan Airport in Boston. It was clear to me that there was nothing for me in Boston anymore. I had no real friends. We had all grown so far apart. My training, education, and life experiences in the past five years had taken me to such a different place. I really needed to look at what I wanted to do with my life. It was a completely open book with no restraints and no responsibilities. That can be more scary than exhilarating.

I had absolutely no idea what I wanted in life, where I wanted to live, or what I wanted to achieve. It was too much freedom all at once with no direction. I knew I needed and wanted to reconnect to my brothers and sister. I decided that to see my brothers and sister I would need to be able to fly. Since I didn't have the finances, I would need to become an airline stewardess. Don't look for logic; it just seemed the natural conclusion. It also seemed like the perfect way to see the world after having been inside the walls all those years. What I have discovered about myself is that I feel most comfortable when I can first get the background and the larger picture of any issue or situation. I feel much better making decisions or particular choices after I have seen it all in perspective. It was so strange to see that just months before I had helped create an international incident by going from Methuen into Lawrence on a bicycle, a 20-minute bike trip, and here I was considering flying in an airplane around the world. I was going to see my brothers and my sister and I intended to get a broader perspective on the world, on life, and all the changes that had taken place since I had left. As frightening as it was, this was life at its finest and most outrageous.

As has happened with so many of my major life decisions, I was walking into the unknown. I had never been in an airplane or even seen one up close but those were the details. It seemed like a logical move. I was going to see the world I had left years before. Not that I had ever seen it before I went in but, hey, I wanted to see it now. I got out the yellow pages and wrote a letter to every single airline in it, asking what to do. I discovered that if you want to fly for a foreign airline you need a foreign passport. I had no idea what a passport was, but if it was important, I wanted one. I asked if I could buy one and then began to learn I really was stepping off a cliff on this one. They initially thought I was kidding but this is how you learn that fact is always so much stranger than fiction. How on earth was I supposed to have learned about passports? We never even had a car until I was 10 and right after high school I went in the convent. World travel was not a specialty. (Can you understand why I have little patience with people who say: "I can't"? Get over it! Reach for the stars, you can do it!) In any event, my nationality eliminated a number of those airlines as possibilities. I decided if I am going to fly, why not go all the way? Why fly domestic if I can fly international? TWA ended up seeming like the best international airline to fly for. You will not believe this one… To fly internationally, I needed a second language. Guess which one? I had French. Little did poor Sr. Alice know about her success story. I had made it in two radically different environments and all because I spoke French, sort of. When you have a dream you can't let ANYTHING get in your way. Those so called obstacles are only details to be dealt with. If it is where you are meant to go, I truly believe that the Holy Spirit works out the issues as you keep your focus on the goal.

In order to get through the acceptance process, and only 4 out of every 100 did, I needed to pass a French test, a personality test, and a weight check. Having been inside the convent where weight really wasn't a priority, I had an extra 30 lbs. to lose. In one month I lost it all, (I would never recommend it now. Now I am smart, then I was a little less so.), studied French, and tried to have my best personality out on testing day. Somehow I made it. Again, if you would only watch the sequence of my life as it unfolds, or yours, you can see the synchronicity in all of it. Who knew where it was all going? Just trust that, if you follow your heart and your soul's longing, you will always end up exactly where you are meant to be. It will always be in that place that works best for your life and the lessons you need to learn. Some lessons, as you will see below, however, you need to learn a few times before they really sink in and so experience repeats itself again and again until you get it.

When it was all set that I would join TWA, I realized I needed to tell my boss, the dean of the business school, that I was leaving. This was hard for me to do since I didn't want to hurt his feelings. Isn't it something, how those of us who are in the developmental stage of care-taking everyone on the planet, are always protecting others from getting their feelings hurt? At that level of development, sadly, our feeling always seem insignificant in comparison. Why on earth I thought he would be devastated by my leaving never ceases to amaze me. In any event, the day before I was going to make my announcement, I was at my desk typing a letter for him. He yelled out of his office asking me to get him a cup of coffee. Since I was busy typing and I could see he was just looking out of the window, I suggested he get it since I was busy. I truly did not say that with any political overtone. I had no hidden agenda. It was just so logical. At the moment, I was busy typing a letter he needed to get out and he was just relaxing. This was a team effort. Well, the next day I went in, all primed to apologize for quitting with "I need to move on, this job just isn't right for me etc. etc." and he called me into his office and asked me to sit down. He began HIS prepared speech about how this just wasn't working. I was feeling terrific because I thought that perhaps now he wouldn't take it so hard that I needed to leave and already had another job. Never having quit a job before, it took me a couple of minutes to realize I was being fired. When I did, I got somewhat indignant and mentioned that he couldn't fire me because I had already decided to quit. Now I was really confused about what I should feel. I hadn't dropped the pity for him yet because I still couldn't figure out if I was fired or if I quit. This is where humor has immense value. We both got what we wanted, we both won, and yet somehow it felt like we both lost and that is a really confusing situation.

The only thing that was certain at the moment was that I was officially an ex-nun, I was no longer a secretary and I was about to undertake an adventure I NEVER would have thought possible back in the days of Southie. A couple months before, as a religious, I certainly had no idea this was coming. I truly hadn't known where I was going - only that I no longer belonged there. Trust, faith, and following your intuitive knowing are the key. I needed this next experience. In my gut I knew there was something for me to do there, I just had no idea what. It wasn't even about my brothers and sister anymore; there was something I needed to do and I needed to find it. I knew that it was only the beginning but it was a necessary first step. I really saw it as a natural progression and yet the ridiculousness of the situation really struck me. Who would believe this level of freedom, these choices, and with no real intellectual reasoning, only an inner knowing that I was being lead and also so clearly that I was co-creating something. I was co-creating my life. It was all so far from anything I had learned. It felt so much like I was living this surreal existence yet I felt more real, more me, than I had ever been in my life. It was truly an adventure. I was reading the book as it went along. I had no idea what the next page would hold but I trusted it would work out. How could it not? Hasn't your life done the same? If you look at it without criticism or blame, what do you see?

I called my girlfriend, explained the entire quitting/firing situation and, when she finally stopped laughing, she told me not to think about it but just clear out my desk and meet her for a drink. The Irish have an amazing ability to think that having a drink makes it all better. In truth, it does at times, especially if you use the time to look at the insanity in another self-made dilemma. It is imperative that we learn very early to laugh at our own craziness. As I have said, I tell my patients often, mental health isn't about having it "all together." Mental health is about understanding your own little touch of craziness. Understanding what your buttons are, and where it is that you lose logic and jump into emotional overreaction and defense. If you can figure that out, it isn't that your issues all disappear, although some do, but many simply lose their ability to affect your behavior or your emotional response. You take your power back. Mental health means understanding and unconditionally loving who you are. Once you have that, everything else is a piece of cake.

When my kids were growing up, I told them often, no matter what happens, it is only a problem. There are no crises; crisis is a mindset. There are just big problems and little problems. Whatever it was, we were family, and we would deal with it together, that's what families are for. My daughter told me just yesterday, for 18 years she hated having a mom who was a shrink; now she couldn't live without it. The way I figure it, for 18 years there was so much she tried to put over on me but it usually didn't work and that ticked her off. Now she can see the unconditional love that has always been there for her and her brother and she now asks for the wisdom age has brought and the insight that can be given without judgment; also now she sees difficulties are just problems. There is nothing so big that she can't tell mom and nothing so bad we can't figure out how to get through it or learn to deal with it. As a teenager it was always a crisis, now it is just a problem. Back then she insisted also that she go through it alone. What a gift for her, to have come to the realization that she doesn't need to go through anything alone, and that nothing is so great it can't be dealt with. How wonderful she could get that at 23, not 43. For all you parents out there who wonder if your children will ever get it, just love them completely and unconditionally. They will, and at some point you become less dumb and less embarrassing.

# Chapter Five
## Life as an Airline Stewardess

*Sometimes a dream can be simply to live.*
*That is living the dream.*

FINALLY, IT WAS TIME TO GO INTO the next phase. When we were ready to go to flight training, TWA sent all of us tickets to fly to Kansas City, Missouri, their home base. Because it was the first time I had ever seen a plane up close, I was frightened and excited about the whole thing. The flight to school was all I could think about. I had no energy to deal with anything else. I prayed that I didn't get plane sick. My sister Mary used to get carsick (although I sometimes wondered if it wasn't just a ploy to get a window seat). With four kids in the back seat and two windows, whatever worked seemed to be the motto. This time, however, it was about the rest of my life, not a window seat. I had given up what I knew and was taking off to do things I had never imagined. I could handle it if it didn't work, but it would be so much easier if it did. I took it as a really good sign when I realized I felt so totally free and alive above the clouds. It was my first plane ride ever and I could just see me working in the galley, talking to passengers, and just loving my life in the air. It was later, after flying for quite a while, that I could express the thought, that it seemed as if I was up there, and any problems or unfinished business I may have had was down there. It was glorious.

As soon as we got to flight school, the process of elimination started. Everyone seemed to come for a different reason. Some wanted to travel, some wanted to get out of their little towns, some wanted to run away, some wanted the illusion of glamour, and some wanted the readily available popularity. One angle I had never thought about was that we were considered to be Sex Goddesses of some kind. I certainly felt rather unqualified for the job. I was three months out of the convent; I wasn't even sexually active, much less a sex Goddess. Illusions are created by people who need them, and, perpetuated by people who profit from them. That was a lesson I learned early in this game. It certainly has caused me to take time to think and assess whether or not I am in illusion when something exciting seems to come up.

In any event, the privileged girls who came to school expecting to become even more elitist, left very quickly when they realized they needed to share a room with someone and they were expected to make their own beds. It amazed me that someone could pack up their life in a suitcase and come to career training and then leave so quickly. Commitment and working hard were not the norm for everyone. After spending five years counting my blessings and acknowledging the strengths and limitations of religious life, I assumed everyone took all their commitments this seriously and never gave up unless all options were tried and the obvious was clear.

We had some very beautiful girls in our class. Initially I felt very intimidated by them. They all seemed to know how to use make-up and all seemed so thin, tall, and gorgeous. We had girls from all 50 states and they all had a different form of beauty to show. We had Hawaiian beauties, young farm girls, and Las Vegas showgirls. It was an introduction to all of American life for me. Having gone from the projects to the convent, my exposure was extremely limited. I discovered, however, as time went on, that I had something to offer as well. Someone had obviously thought I looked and fit the part or I wouldn't have been hired in the first place.

As the students discovered I was an ex-nun, I found more and more women coming to my room at night. Some were looking for forgiveness and absolution for past abortions or past affairs. Some needed a solid shoulder to cry on. I realized that my ministry, which I thought took place in the convent and with the poor, actually could take place anywhere. There were so many poor souls out there, filled with pain who needed the understanding and unconditional love we had learned to give. It made sense that I had been led to religious life to find out who I was and to see all the gifts of ministry that existed. It felt as if I was born to be in ministry, but the only approach I had known as a child, for a woman, was as a Catholic nun and that wasn't where I belonged. A whole new world of possibilities was opening up for me along with a whole new interpretation of what it meant to be who I was called to be.

Ministry is simply loving unconditionally and leading people home to their own soul's essence. It can be done anywhere, in any context. What I see, is that who we are is what we bring to our ministry. It isn't about what we have learned or who we know, or what titles we carry; it is about who we are and how able we are to let the essence of our own soul radiate out. In that sense, we are all called to minister and all in different ways. At that point, I became the standard shoulder to cry on. I was rarely informed about an existing affair. It was usually a past one that had left them in guilt. The present one, students wanted to hide. Perhaps I could send them to hell as quickly as I could forgive them? Whatever the case, so many students saw me as the church personified, for all the good and the bad that it stood for. In all of that, I found a place where I could do my ministry but not much of a place for me, a woman in cultural shock. I felt so alone. The developing sense that I was called to keep my ministry, just transform it, appealed to me immensely. It allowed me to see this experience in a context in which I didn't feel misplaced. Even if I had been asked to leave at that point I would have felt that I got what I had come there for. I rediscovered my ministry and its true meaning and it felt so right. I was beginning to feel solid again, even if alone and in a strange land. I had left religious life and there was no going back. With the excitement of understanding ministry in a new way and finding another avenue for doing service and soul connection, I never realized I was still missing a part of the puzzle. It would take decades before I could learn to ask for what I needed and yet what I gave so readily. Ministering to others was natural; self-ministry was another life lesson that was much harder to learn.

In flight school, there were several situations set up to wean out any that they thought couldn't do the job. I had learned earlier that only 4 out of every 100 that applied to the school got accepted, but I also learned that for every student who made it through flight school, another two didn't. We were a select group to finish. We had a thing called "fright flight." In it a plane was set to go to a certain altitude and stall, intentionally. No one knew about this so it was a shocker to those of us in that plane. Some panicked and once the plane landed they walked off and kept on walking. I figured, after all I had been through, it was only a problem. If we crashed, I would handle it. Whatever the circumstances were, I would deal. If I died, there was nothing to deal with and I would just go home to Spirit. It wasn't all that complicated. I must say, however, I was very grateful I stayed home the night before as recommended. Those who had gone out drinking and dancing used a lot of the sick bags. That was an experience I did not want at all.

Another day we had a simulated fire on the airplane. We had to evacuate everyone down the slides. On a 747, we could evacuate 365 people in less than 60 seconds. It was really quite impressive. Unfortunately, some panicked here, also, and were asked to leave. For me, the hardest part was in learning that, in an emergency, some people go into such denial that they will not stop reading their magazine. We needed to leave those people to die, if necessary, since we couldn't risk losing a plane full of people in order to save a few. That was a tough one since it was in my early childhood that I began trying to save everyone, even the dad I pitied and hated at times.

It was in this school that I had my first encounter with the weight pathology of the western culture. You could be eliminated from the program if you were ½ lb. overweight at any check-in. We had gorgeous showgirls let go because of weight. It made no sense to me. I had been so skinny growing up that I had saved my nickel allowance each day so that on Saturday I could go to the drugstore and get a hot fudge sundae hoping I would gain ten pounds that day. I wanted breasts and hips and everything else those girls had. Now they were eliminated. It made absolutely no sense. We had no salt shakers in the dining room since that caused you to retain water. There were no high fat foods available. All of this was good but the reasoning was lacking a little. The focus in the last half of class was on weight and tests. I never realized before that we were expected to get a 98% average on all our tests, so that was where my focus went. Yet again, I made it, and was accepted into the ranks. This time it was the ranks of the TWA airline stewardesses.

Those of us who were going to fly internationally, stayed after the rest of our classmates graduated. We spent weeks learning about evacuations over water and whatever other specific information applied to international flights and customs, etc. Those flying the European route, who wanted to, stayed another week to learn how to work on the 747's. They were the brand new planes out and TWA was the only airline to have any. I wasn't about to miss out on anything at this point. I had come this far, why stop now? Also, it had begun to feel safe in school. I always did well there. Being out, "in the world," was feeling more frightening every day. Eventually, we all had to graduate and go to our assignments. I was sent to New

York City and Kennedy Airport. By that point in time, I could light a cigarette in 23 steps even if I didn't smoke. I could walk up and down any flight of stairs I came to, just like a lady, and I could apply make-up and false eyelashes. In addition, I could help evacuate an airplane in 60 seconds and serve a great meal in first class or coach. It was all in a day's work. I was ready to face the passengers, I think. I had no idea, whatsoever, about New York City and the life ahead, but I would learn, in ways I never knew.

After our final graduation, we all left in shifts. Those of us who were going to Kennedy Airport in New York City all left at about the same time. The airlines had recommended a particular hotel for us for the first few days while we looked for apartments, etc. Some of us got there early and discovered that prostitutes worked in the lobby. Because many of us were wearing makeup and false eyelashes for the first time, as well as never having been in a city anything like New York, we were green and flaunting it. We were the perfect bait for the sharks. After a few flabbergasted "No"s , we all found other places to stay. It was amazing to me, that just a few months ago my life had been so predictable and my "outrageous" behavior, which caused a scandal, would be laughed at now. There are times when it is so hard to take in all the things that can occur in such a short time. I thought I was in cultural shock before, but I soon learned I hadn't even begun that experience yet.

In trying to find a place to stay, I hooked up with a classmate who was from Boston as well. We had talked a few times in flight school but had never really gotten close. She didn't know anyone else and really hadn't gotten close to anyone in school either. We got along reasonably well and we were both in a strange world so we decided it was better to have a partner than try to do this alone. Roaches and vermin of all sorts were overrunning all the apartments we called.

It was quite an introduction to the glamorous world other people thought we lived in.

There is a thing in New York City called a "stew zoo." They are apartment buildings pretty well taken over by stews and flight crew. Every apartment seemed to have 5-6 stews. We all worked different schedules so if your roommate worked six days straight on the international double-shift, her bed was free during that time. As long as you were willing to share your bed and your dresser with others, it worked. It cut expenses immensely because it allowed a lot of people to live in a very small apartment. You just chose a flight schedule that was opposite your roommate's (or bed mate's in some circumstances). Also, flight people live in their own subculture. It is a way of life most people only dream about. "I can't come to your dinner party Thursday night; I am going to be in Rome." After a long trip we used to get together at a crew-member's house just onto Long Island. We would plan it in Rome, Paris, Geneva, or Madrid, wherever we were the day before. We would all buy something in that country to bring to the dinner party. It all seemed so "normal" after a while. All this and we were making wages that qualified us for food stamps. It all became a surreal way of life. All of this was happening just after leaving the convent and a semi-cloistered life-style. Strangely, in trying to find a place in this world, I, like so many others, needed to try out so many varied possibilities before I could discover what felt fully like home for me. For too many people, so much of life is filled with the mundane and unexpected aspects of life.

We can make life a boring experience of struggle or an exciting excursion into the unknown filled with self-discovery while also developing the ability to love others fully and unconditionally. From my perspective, there was only one way of living that could fill me and call me forward, and it required my full participation and reaching for the stars. At that moment, it entailed looking for a place to live. In any event, after looking at a few of the stew zoos, we both decided we did not want to share our beds with others, or even our bedrooms. I had met a guy at a party in Boston just before I left for flight school and he had offered to let me stay at his place until I found a place to stay. I called him up, in my ex-nun innocence, and mentioned our predicament. He and his roommate were more than willing to have two stews stay there for a while. Little did I know what we were getting into. Linda was much more a "woman of the world" than I was, so she just assumed I was OK with everything. When you don't expect to see things, you usually don't and I didn't. What I did notice was that the place needing cleaning. So the first day, while the guys were at work and before we went apartment hunting, I scrubbed and cleaned the fridge, the floor, the shower, and everything else I could get my hands on. This, to me, was my thank-you for a place to stay. It was later on that things started getting quite clear. The guys had moved into one bedroom and we had the other. They let that ride for a week or two and when we still couldn't find an affordable apartment anywhere they decided they needed to move back into their own bedrooms and so we would each sleep with one of them. Having had three brothers, I didn't see a problem when you are in this kind of a situation. By the next morning, we expanded our search to far beyond Manhattan.

I find it an honest to God miracle I am not dead or worse. Having come from the projects, I had this self-image of a woman who knew the world and the streets. At times my mother would tell me she was frightened by certain looks I gave her. Having gone into religious life, however, it seemed as if I had lost any and all sense of street smarts. It was as if I had never had a single one. The value systems that I had come to adopt so fully, and made my own, were so radically different from those of the city. It was as if I had never known any other. I had been so completely transformed that I no longer had the defense or world view of the girl I had been. I was now a woman who had just left religious life and I was in the lion's den.

In my own defense, I went into the convent at 17, straight from high school. Being tough meant handling gangs of kids my own age and knowing when the cops would come. I had never hurt a soul and I usually had a boyfriend whose parents were as strict as my dad, so our "acting out" was very limited. At this point, in New York City, I felt completely defenseless. I had absolutely no idea how the world worked. I was no longer kissing teenage boys; I was now fighting off stockbrokers and analysts. I had never even met one before and I certainly didn't own any stock. Linda and I quickly found an apartment in Flushing, Queens. It was the upstairs of a two family house. I went out and bought a very inexpensive bedroom set and we pitched in to buy a kitchen set and some small appliances. For the big pieces, we waited until garbage day and just walked the streets looking for couches and chairs. It was an adventure and we enjoyed it. Because neither one of us had ever had our own place before, it was all so much fun and felt very grown-up and sophisticated. My large black trunk from the convent, covered with cloth, served as the entertainment center, which held the TV and stereo system we had found in the garbage. It really was a very pretty apartment. We sprayed everything we discovered on our garbage days for bugs, left them outside on the porch for a few days, and then they were as good as new, at least as far as we were concerned.

Because there was a third bedroom, we found a third roommate. This was an experience. She had a good heart but she was fairly vacant on top. I may have been naïve beyond words in the male department but I had great strengths in organization and implementation of a plan. Sue, well, she had never even made a bed before.

We were definitely from different worlds. Because my parents both worked, it was my job to make sure all the beds were made, dinner was cooked, and the younger ones were OK. In our house, the three oldest took turns after dinner, cleaning the table, washing the dishes, and drying. It was natural. The biggest problem was remembering who did what last week. This girl had never washed a dish. I never even thought someone could reach 20 without knowing certain basic things. Linda and I had an adventure in store. We also discovered how irate Sue got if we expected her to pass up on a great sale just to pay the rent. There was always "next week." She was a California girl and she probably should have stayed there.

One of the greatest thrills for me at the time was the ability to fly all over the world, wherever I chose. I explored parts of this world country by country, people by people. I learned the people of each country have a unique energy all their own. They are as solidly a reflection of that country as are the landscape, the architecture, and the arts. I realized how much I love people and how our illusions of right and wrong are so narrow and limiting. People and places are different from us, not better or worse, just different. What an absolutely freeing realization! I could just love and accept people for who they were – being intrigued by their habits and patterns without needing to find a box to put them in, without needing to judge. I didn't have a long- range dream for my future yet I was content with knowing about, and living, this aliveness and this freedom. Although this was the experience I had longed for so many years ago, I had no idea what it would look like, what context this living life to its fullest would be in. Even at that, it was clear to me on some level that I was in a temporary stage of my life while I was preparing and growing for whatever lay ahead.

Some of the experiences taught me so much about me that I had never realized before. On one flight a front door started squealing at about 36,000 feet high. I talked to the steward (who was making more than me simply because he had a penis) and he said he wasn't going out first and so he went to sit in the back of the plane. I phoned the captain who came down to inspect it. We lowered our altitude and everything was fine. He said that happens sometimes. (WHAT????) I sat there wondering how this all happened. Here I was, sitting in a first class jump seat between servings and my flight partner was in the back of the plane. I faced the trouble and made it better simply by dealing with it. I hadn't dealt with this since I left my father's house. I began to see that whenever we had an emergency, I always readily jumped in and handled things. I stayed calm, dealt with the problem, and got everything back to normal as much as possible. It was when I got back to my apartment that I started to babble and eat lots of chocolate cake. Knowing my pattern let me feel so much saner and even alive. I had stopped surviving and was now learning, and growing and living. My dream had become a reality on so many levels. I could see things so clearly at that point. I had made it. I just had to keep telling myself that.

In one emergency landing we needed to have the runway foamed since it seemed the landing gear would not come down. After a few moments of inner terror, if not panic, I just took a deep breath and dealt with everything that needed to be done while some of the folks around me talked about not making enough money to have to deal with this while others simply went silent. There were always those of us who just did what needed to be done. My training at my father's house proved very worthwhile. I never realized I was being trained for the future; I thought I was just surviving the past. My love of people, and the realization that we were all different not better, made some trips quite funny. You never knew what you would run into. There were always the business men who asked us to tighten their seat belts and the pregnant mothers who wanted the first class leftovers since they were still hungry. Tours were always fun. People were just out to play and laugh. They could pick on each other in a way only folks who knew each well could do. Hugging a stew, or having a picture taken with one, was a big deal for some and boy did it bring a lot of jokes from their friends. Things that were done innocently, and with respect, were always fine; it helped them have better memories of the trip to take home. It was fun making people happy and helping them end their vacation on a high note.

We also met some very interesting people. On one flight in first class to London I met an interesting man who was an African ambassador to the UN. He was going to visit his cousin who was an African delegate to England. My brother Bob had taught in Zambia, Africa so I found the continent intriguing after all his stories. I was invited to dinner at the embassy and really felt I had come up in the world. My friends all had interesting stories to tell and many were as innocent as mine. It was just such an interesting experience to meet so many different people from all over the world and all walks of life. One friend was invited to an extravagant event but didn't have appropriate clothing so this passenger took her out to get an entire outfit. It is amazing that it is the sleazes who expect to be repaid with sex. The men of class simply want company they enjoy. The hard part was taking a chance since you never really knew who was who. I tended to play it safe (remember everything is relative) and just went out with the crew. We would go to plays in England, out to dance in Germany, to great restaurants in Paris and so on. We developed routines. We shopped during the day, took a nap, and then went out at night. It was so very different from anything I had ever known. It was a dream yet it could get old. When you listen within, you know when it is time to do something different. It was getting to be about that time. I wanted to start dating and have someone special in my life. All these new experiences seemed as if they would be so much more fun if I could share them with someone special.

# Chapter Six
## Dating

*Sometimes dreams are based on illusions.*
*They can be a product of our fears or our innocence.*

SINCE LEAVING RELIGIOUS LIFE I HAD DATED very little. There was so much to see and do and so very much to learn about me and about life. Anyway, I felt very awkward. It seemed everyone had so much more finesse than I did. In religious life I had grown intellectually and spiritually; however, socially I was still 17 when I left. Our community talked about 1 hour a day unless required to speak. That did not demand a lot of social skills so very few were developed. Who had the time or the chance for experience? Besides, we were nuns. No one thinks of a social life with a nun. Nuns just are. I remember a student once asking me if nuns ate or if they went the bathroom. I told him no, we just prayed. I thought it was hysterical. I have no idea where he went with that.

Being an ex-nun brought equally ignorant comments, usually around dating. Carol had had a friend who said he always wanted to sleep with a nun. He may still be trying.....Unfortunately, to this day I still hear that desire and it has been a long time since that title fit. Although Carol, my old high school friend, and I double dated a few times, it was so uncomfortable I hated it. They were men she knew. I had no idea what to say. I had spent all those years without a radio, television, newspaper, or magazine so I really wasn't up on anything. I wanted to be sophisticated but felt like a country bumpkin. When we went dancing, the only things I knew were the "oldies but goodies." I went in when the Beatles sang "I Want To Hold Your Hand." I came out after they had broken up. I knew Motown but came out to the Mamas and the Papas. I was in throughout the Vietnam demonstrations. I left in one world and came out to another. I thought having a boyfriend would be a great idea but the process of finding one and dating seemed too hard.

When Bearings got me that very short-lived job at Boston College, I met a man, John, who was a senior at the time. He was in and out of the dean's office often since he was president of this and chairman of that. He didn't have a lot of experience dating either. He and I dated during my very brief period at Boston College. I then took off for Kansas City for flight training. When I moved to Flushing, he would come and visit us. He and Linda got along very well so we all hung out together. Once Rich moved in "temporarily," we had a foursome since Sue was usually off with a boyfriend. After graduation from college, John soon took off for Europe to be a "Ski Bum" with three of his friends. They had all decided that they would be working for the rest of their lives so it made sense that they spend their first post-college year doing what they loved. Skiing their way across Europe was just that. We wrote on occasion and at times I called if I was in the same country as he was. We were dating but in an obviously limited way. It was more like developing a friendship over time. I liked it like that. A friendship needed to develop before a healthy "couple" relationship could begin, if it was going to.

In the meantime, when John wasn't around, I attended weekly meetings of Bearings in New York City to help me adjust to all the changes in my life. What I discovered, though, was that a number of priests would attend, who had no intention of leaving the priesthood, but they loved meeting new ex-nuns. It was like fresh meat had just hit the streets and the wolves were out. I dated one man a few times, platonically, and was always flabbergasted that he would borrow a parishioner's car so we could go out. He talked of a trip to the Bahamas but it was all so surreal to me. He was playing with fire but I was the one who felt guilty. I realized I couldn't do this. It went against everything I believed in. It went against my integrity. It was so convoluted I couldn't reconcile it all with who I was choosing to be. I wanted to simplify my life and keep it uncluttered spiritually and emotionally and this was all too much. Being single, without a relationship, was so much simpler.

It isn't that I necessarily made any better choices but they were made with a clear conscience and were done in ignorance or naiveté not malice or lack of integrity. Because of my idealism, I assumed everyone held the same ideals that I did. I believed everyone wanted the best for everyone else. It wasn't long before I realized otherwise. In London, a crew member had asked me out for dinner. I went and we had a good time seeing the sights since he had been there so often and we had dinner at a nice restaurant. After, he seemed to become rather obnoxious and I couldn't understand the change. Only later did it dawn on me that he figured, since he bought dinner I would go to bed with him. As if accepting one invitation was approval for all others. Thankfully, the next day, I had the nerve to ask another stewardess about this and you could see by that look in her eye that she felt I was a hopeless case about to be devoured by the masses. After she explained the rules of the game, she also informed me he was notorious for doing this. Everyone avoided him for just that reason. We had so many pilots who said they were married in Texas, or this state or that, but that they worked in Paris or Madrid wherever. At least they were up front about it. In the beginning, I thought they were teasing. I had this idealistic belief that if a man got married, he was so in love with his wife that he would never even look at another woman but I learned otherwise.

As happened so often, I learned the hard way. When a gorgeous copilot asked me out, I was ecstatic. I figured this is it. He was gorgeous, warm, friendly, natural, and so easy to be with. After bidding the same flights for a while and traveling to so many countries together, it seemed OK to get involved. The whole crew always stayed in the same hotel so it was so convenient. While we were in his bed for the first time, this man casually mentioned, while we were discussing nature and the outdoors, that when he was leaving his home that morning he looked back and could see his wife and daughter in the forefront and all his horses behind. It was a glorious view. I just stayed there stunned while he had no idea he had said anything ungentlemanly, if not down-right horrific. I slowly got up and then ran across the hall to my room. It was about two months before I got over the shock. He tried to corner me to talk, to explain, to do whatever, and I couldn't even look at him. I couldn't believe he would do such a thing. What about loving his wife and never going to another? What about his vows? What about me? What about us? I was now fully present, here, in the lay world. It ran through every cell of my body. I had no idea what to do or how to handle any of this. There was no one else in my shoes. No other ex-nun saying "WHAT"? What world am I living in? What planet am I on? The others had all dealt with this long before. When I asked one woman who flew many of the same routes I did, if this ever happened to her, she left me flabbergasted. She told me she only dated married men. Single men become too clingy. Married men are afraid of losing you so they always buy you nice presents, take you to nice restaurants, and take you on wonderful trips. They have to spend time with their wives and kids so you get a lot of free time to do what you want or even nothing at all because nobody lives with you, they just visit. For the major holidays you can fly home and visit with family and no one is telling you that, you have to see their side this time. Needless to say, this left me numb. This was cultural shock at its finest…

It had been quite a year. I had faced losing the only lifestyle I had lived in as an adult. I left a loving, safe environment where we all had the same basic values, we just all wanted to live them in different ways. I had a "coming out of the convent" party in a bar and vomited the whole way home, drunk on one drink. I had a friend trying to convince me to go on the pill a few days after leaving the convent. I had applied to flight school when it was obvious I was not a secretary. I had gone through flight school, moved to New York, dealt with male roommates, found an apartment and furnished it on garbage day, and dealt with some men who would buy dinner or a drink and then expect a full night of God knows what. I then started to fall in love with a married man who cheated on his wife and talked about it in bed as if he was discussing the weather, and now a "friend" was telling me the only sane way to date was to date married men. I definitely was not ready for life as an adult in the lay world. I had absolutely no idea where to go next or even how to get there. I was totally lost and putting one foot in front of the other, wondering how it was I got home or got to work. It was all way, way, way too much. It took a few months of numbness and shock to realize my entire value system was thrown into the air. I knew one thing; if I were ever going to date again I would make sure he was single. There was only one man I knew for certain was single. He still lived with his mother even though he was skiing in Switzerland at the moment. Going through life alone seemed so much like a minefield. Living my dream was bringing up all the other details of my life I hadn't dealt with yet. (I have learned that that is to be expected, no matter where we are on our journey.) It was clearly time to do more inner work.

John and I had continued to write on occasion, and when I was in Geneva, long after this fiasco was over, he would come to my hotel from Zermatt for the night. We got along well and he seemed to have softened from his time away. He had been brusque and impatient at times in the states and rather egocentric. His time away caused some softening; I assumed it was maturity. In time, we started talking about a future. Because John and his friends had been living in Zermatt, Switzerland, and were now thinking about going home, he decided it would make sense for us to get married and for him to come back to the states now. I was more in favor of living together first but he felt that went against his Catholic values. As I said, after I left religious life, religious values seemed to hold little weight for me. I trusted my own sense of rightness and my sincerity and innate goodness. I knew I loved God and all the people I met, even those who had thrown me for a loop. I also could see that those people who were so negative, angry, and belligerent were usually good folks who were in pain. I lived in integrity, tried to love and honor everyone I met, and spread joy wherever I could. I was living my faith daily and didn't feel the need to profess it in a church. John, however, was adamant and I wanted to respect his religious beliefs.

On that trip when John had come to my room and decided we should be married, I had been out of the convent about a year. I didn't have extensive experience with men and I certainly didn't have much of a sense of the world and what it entailed. What I knew was that, when he was sober, I enjoyed his company. Living in Zermatt brought out a side of his personality that was so wonderful, so gentle, so sincere, and so real. If he wanted to get married, sure, why not? It seemed as if he had grown so much and had let go of so much of his anger and hostility. It seemed that he had changed. It was as if he had found an inner peace that permeated his whole life. I had begun to feel the longing for someone special, for someone to live with and be with. It seemed like great timing.

As a romantic and money saving adventure, we decided to go to Amsterdam to buy my diamond. It is filled with diamond factories that cut and polish any diamond you choose. As I look back on it, so many years later, I see that John was frightened of being alone when he went back to the states and I so much wanted someone to love. We filled the base minimum requirements of what we each wanted. We liked each other somewhat and we both wanted to be in love so we fell in love. It can be easy to convince yourself that like is love when love is what you need and want. I believe we both saw the intrinsic goodness in the other and we wanted that in our lives, so we grabbed on and held on tight.

Before we could go to Amsterdam, however, I first needed to take my flight back to New York since it was a round trip flight for the crew. I flew back to Kennedy, landed around 2:00 in the afternoon, applied for a pass to Geneva for the 7:00 flight that night, and traded flights with a friend so I could have time off now and take her flight later in the month. I then went home to get clothes for a week or so and got back to the airport to take my flight. As I said, the life of a stew is very different from most others. When I arrived in Geneva, I got the Cog Railroad to take me to Zermatt. The next day we left to go to Amsterdam for the diamond, by train. It was all very romantic and like a fairy tale. There was something surreal about it but I wanted to be in love so that is what I was going to feel. Coming into Amsterdam and seeing the tulips, for as far as the eye could see, was exquisite. It was just so beautiful. My tendency to be more laid back and John's to get things done "right," kept coming up, but as so many of us do, I just passed it off as "nerves." I didn't want to see anything that wasn't wonderful so, consequently, I just didn't see it. Denial is a phenomenal tool for those who use it well.

After I got my diamond, we came back to the states and six weeks later we got married on Mother's Day. It was the only date available in the next several months for a hall to be open for a reception. John rushed to find a job and I rushed to get the wedding organized. It all came together and it went beautifully. It was all still surreal, and I had the strangest feelings while walking down the aisle. I was to find out later how common those feelings really are. I realized I did not know this man. I also realized this marriage would make me whole, real, and powerful or it would kill me. I decided as I was walking down the aisle to take a chance.

It amazes me that once a couple decides to get married, it is as if all the awareness, all the dating, all the meaningful talks that allow you to continue getting to know one another stop. You get consumed in wedding plans, the wedding takes precedence, and your relationship is put on the back burner. You try to stay out of each other's way, all the while pretending you are doing this together. I am all for potluck weddings in the backyard. The whole reception concept is to share your commitment with the community, in a community gathering. Relax. Because of the pre-wedding pace, walking down the aisle for many is the first time they have had a chance to think and feel. Those feelings that may have come up earlier, if you had slowed down, come up then. It is the rare woman, or man, who has the ability to say, "Hey, wait a minute, I need to think about this a little more." You have spent thousands of dollars, everyone is here, and the reception is being set up as you stand there so. . . . There is a belief, I think, that "I can make this work." "I can love enough for the two of us." "I can get him/her to see how blessed s/he is in having me." They are all wishes made with the best of intentions and usually followed by years of effort, and denial.

It is a very common theme for the women I have spoken to, both professionally and personally, that on their wedding day, when they were walking down the aisle, they had a realization. It has been described often as a sensation that went through them that this could be the best day of their life or the beginning of a very difficult time. Many such as with myself have no idea where to go with that realization so they go forward. Wedding planners never take that reality into consideration. As I said, I knew, in a split second, from out of nowhere, that this marriage would make me or break me. I had no idea which. Unfortunately, we have not been taught to listen to our own inner knowing. So many of us have been taught to trust appropriate behavior and we do, even when it goes against our intuitive sense of what is right or wrong.

Although much of this is changing, for everyone, it is usually done with mixed emotions and uncertainty. People are still looking for the ONE right way to do this or that. THERE ISN'T ONE. In terms of marriage, each couple comes together in their unique way, with so much junk from their families, and their past relationships, with all the pain, abandonment fears, insecurities, and self-questioning they possess. Each partner also comes with their own natural and developed strengths, none better or worse than the others, just different. If each couple could just take the time, before marriage, to take a look and figure out, without judgment, who is bringing what to this relationship? Not who is bringing more and who less? But how is it all going to fit together? What help will we need, objectively, to put all this to good use and provide a fertile ground for the relationship to grow? It is so important and yet so uncommon for such a thing to occur. We didn't do it. I don't know many of our generation who did.

How many couples believe they will figure it out when it comes up? Trouble is, when it comes up, there are so many fears and egos involved, objectivity is out of the question and we are all set up for the pain and destruction that will take place because we weren't prepared. It is in this final stage of dating that so much of what is needed to define this relationship, and to see if it can truly become a healthy viable long-term relationship, needs to take place. Every marriage needs to be different because each individual and each couple is different.

For so many people, dating is about grabbing someone to marry when in truth it needs to be seen as a time when we learn so much about ourselves, our tendencies, our limitations, our strengths, and our needs. We need to learn how we react and how we relate in a relationship. It can be so different from what we intellectually believe. Not dating often, leads us to marry with so little self-awareness and so little understanding of what it means to be in a relationship with someone who may be so different from ourselves. Dating can be a scary adventure where we confront all of our insecurities, but it is a necessary part of the preparation for making a life-long decision in partnership. What an experience it has become in a culture where things happen so fast or where it is used as an excuse to use and abuse so many. It is the stage of preparation for marriage and self-awareness. We have so much to learn, especially if we are to make an intelligent decision about a life-long partner who will grow with us while supporting us and the family unit we hope to create together.

# Chapter Seven
## Marriage

*Living your dream can be quite different from dreaming it.*
*Dreams are the beginning of the rest of our lives.*

MY HUSBAND WAS A GOOD MAN AT heart. He wanted so much to have all his dreams come true. He was very structured and very exact about mostly everything. My bottom line belief is that he was filled with so much fear that, from his perspective, everything in his life, and mine, needed to be under his control if it was going to work and he could feel safe. He couldn't imagine failure. He was blessed and cursed. He was almost thirty before he had his first real failure and, consequently, he had absolutely no idea how to handle it. The idea that it is the successful man that has many failures because he has tried many things was not considered at all. To John, that man was simply a failure. It left no room for his humanity or mine. An anxiety-wracked man who worked in insurance had replaced the playful, warm man I had consented to marry in Switzerland. The more frightened he became, the more controlling he became. Within the first six months of our marriage, I came to see that he loved me as completely as he could love. I also came to see that each one of us has a very different capacity for loving. I was so grateful to be loved to any extent, that that became enough, at least for a time. The first clear indicator, for me, about the dynamics of my marriage came only a few months later.

After one of my flights, I went alone to our local grocery store to do the shopping for the week. John had helped make the list. I made the mistake of buying a type of cookie he felt was much too expensive. He insisted that I take it back instantly and buy a cheaper kind. We were not going to waste money in this house! I knew that was a turning point in the marriage, and a decisive point in how we would do things. I knew we were talking about $1.00 or so, nothing of any real significance. I understood clearly, however, that this was about who is in charge here. From my perspective, there was no one person in charge. We were a team. When I mentioned it, John said, "in every team there is a Captain and a water boy - both are needed." Guess who was which? I could see that on one hand, my healthier side perhaps, that I needed to set the precedence now, so that from the beginning, the roles were defined. I also saw this little boy who was struggling to be the man and my heart went out to him. (That became the seducer that supported me in self-betrayal for the duration of my marriage.) I could see it all so clearly, so intelligently, and so logically. I also felt that I would die if he just walked out the door. As I sat with what I felt, not with what I knew, I felt terror. Terror that if he knew he married a woman as strong as he was, or even stronger, as so many would say over the years, he would leave. I had married him. I saw his goodness, his core essence, and the wondrous qualities he possessed. I was a Catholic and I had committed to loving him until death do us part. Most importantly, I had made the decision to love this man with my whole heart and soul. I was falling in love with my husband and I wanted to protect him from his pain no matter how much it caused me. It was the only way I knew how to love. It was how I had loved my whole family, even my dad. For me, loving meant protecting those you cared about. It meant keeping them from their fears and their pain so that you could help them live in their joy and their happiness. At that point, I thought him loving me was about him appreciating all that I was doing and loving my willingness to do it. When his pain was all gone, when I had taken it all away, he would then be able to love me and see all my other qualities of strength and joy and laughter, etc. He would cherish me, I knew he would, or at least I dreamed he would. This was my chance to finally be loved beyond words, forever, to have the security and the comfort I so desperately wanted in my life. I had to hold onto it. It is amazing how our head can know so much, and so clearly, and then our emotions, our fears can come into play and we forget all that we know. Our fears then govern our decisions.

Because of the terror of losing him, I gave in. I walked back to the store and returned the cookies. Throughout that entire walk, I knew I had betrayed myself beyond words. I knew I had defeated my own position in this relationship and that I had helped support the destruction of any possibility of a good, healthy marriage. We had begun the downhill slide before we even had a chance. All this happened because of his terror of not being in control and my terror of being abandoned and unloved. It is fear that destroys so many marriages that may have succeeded. I see it again and again and again. It is usually a fear that is so great neither person can even identify it. It takes on a life of its own and becomes so monstrous, that just the thought of looking at it is terrifying. In the midst of all that, good, loving, well-intentioned people try to make a marriage work. It is so sad to see. It is like watching two young souls trying to push back a mountain with their bare hands.

In a marriage that has good intentions, you get to see the soul, the essence of your partner, even if only rarely. Because of that, I don't know that we ever stop loving the person we were so in love with once. It is such a gift to be able to see the core essence of someone's soul, to see who they really are when they take a moment to stand, undefended, in your presence. Some people choose to live that way as a way of life. Some people only experience it in themselves or their partner, briefly, once or twice in a lifetime. To be able to do that, we first need to let go of that protective anger and resentment that is held against the partner and ourselves. Staying angry and hateful is a safe way not to have to feel all the pain and hurt but it also prevents us from feeling real love and connection. I know that until the day I die, in a small way, I will be in love with my ex-husband. It doesn't mean that I am incapable of loving another; only that I will always be in love with that man I married. He was a man who had such innocence and such passion for life. He had such a joy inside and such gentleness. They only came out, however, when he was totally relaxed, which was rare. He had talked at one time of teaching the mentally and emotionally handicapped to ski. He loved it and wanted to share it with others. That is the man who became the father of my two children. Only later did I see that the "other" man would be the man who came to stay.

The first year we were married, we traveled on my passes as an airline stewardess. We had flown to Portugal first class for our honeymoon. It cost us $10 a piece. We traveled to Florida, Hawaii, Chicago anywhere we had an opportunity or an urge. The next year we saved for a down payment on a house. The following year we saved to buy furniture and appliances. We then bought the house and the following year we saved in order to have money in the bank for when I quit work to stay home with the children. We had it all arranged and in order, in a very practical way. It was not how it started.

It was during our first year of our marriage that I desperately wanted a child and he felt we weren't ready. The second year he was considering it and I felt I needed to prove to myself that I could make it in the business world in case something ever happened to him. I had quit the airlines because our planes kept getting hijacked to the desert in the Middle-East, or, we were dealing with bomb threats. Either way, it wasn't relaxing for me and John never knew if I would come home alive. As a result, I took a job in the same insurance company where he worked. It allowed us to have just one car and to save that much more for our future. By the time I knew

I could make it anywhere, I was ready and we followed our plan perfectly.

We moved from a wonderful apartment with a swimming pool and tennis courts that had been close to the airport for my commuting, to a raised ranch home on a dead end street. We had been so careful in the house we chose. The driveway went down a hill so that if the future children rode bikes down a hill they would end up in the back lawn, not on the street. We had a lot of land so that they could play ball at home and not need to go far. They could also play downstairs in the family room and make all the noise and mess they wanted while we stayed upstairs and close by, if needed. I had my window over the kitchen sink and we had a bathroom upstairs and down. We had lots of land to grow all our own vegetables and to have beautiful landscaping which I loved to work with. Our first night there, we went from the lawyer's office to our new home. The furniture would be delivered the next day so we slept in a sleeping bag on the living room floor, dreaming and talking about all our plans for this home, the things we would fix up or change, and the family we would create in it.

When I became pregnant with Amy Lynn, my first child, I was so happy I was beyond words. Unlike so many women, I loved being pregnant. I couldn't imagine anything better in the whole world. I spent all those months with at least one hand on my belly thinking, I am having a baby, I have a baby in there, I am having a baby.......
To say she was wanted is such an understatement. Those first few months I had morning sickness. But I was pregnant. John and I were both in awe at this experience. It was something to behold. My pregnancy and my marriage consumed my life. I had dreamed of having children when I was in high school, but this far-surpassed anything I could ever imagine. I was filled with such gratitude, such joy, and such thanksgiving. As excited as I got about my pregnancy, I saw

my husband getting a little more apprehensive. Perhaps the awareness of more responsibility was more than he could, or wanted, to
handle. It is amazing how so often mothers and fathers can see and
experience things so differently.

Once I finally went into labor for 18 hours, we were ready to
practice everything they had taught us at Lamaze class. Spot fixation
saved me. I was so frightened at one point when, after 12 hours,
they said, it appears as if labor has stopped. I told them I would
camp in but they were not sending me home. I was not going anywhere. I was so uncomfortable I thought I would die if I moved. I
had gained 50 lbs. during the pregnancy and after 12 hours of labor
I felt like a beached whale lying on that table with my feet in stir-
rups. With me feeling this poorly, I was not very adaptable.

This child wanted to come out and I was going to have all the
medical help I needed readily available when it did. It is something
how we can be so sweet and submissive, such an invalidation of our
truth, and yet so strong when things called for it. Isn't it something,
as well, how strong we can be in fighting for someone else in a way
we could never fight for ourselves? I wanted my child to have the
best from the second she chose to come out and she was going to
have it. Feeling so awful only gave me the inner strength to insist
upon it even more than I normally would.

When I was in religious life, we used to do an exercise called
"examination of conscience" at the end of each day. In those days,
it was to look over how many faults or sins we had committed that
day. I now do it but with the intent of looking over my day, from
the moment I awake, to see in what way, if at all, I invalidated myself, or, my truth. It is a great way, without judgment, to just look
and see in what way we are most prone to invalidate who we have
become. It is a wonderful way to look at how you live your life and

how it is that you find ways to give up who you are and why. Do you lie about your needs in order not to appear needy? Do you appear powerless in order not to make someone else feel insecure? Do you appear unknowing in order to help someone feel in charge and knowledgeable? There are so many ways we betray ourselves. Having a so-called good intention is no reason or justification for such behavior. Do you lie about your wants in order not to appear "selfish"? I have discovered, so-called "selfish-people" never feel selfish; they can justify every need and want ten times over if they need to. It is the person who never gives themselves permission to have a need that appears selfish in their own eyes when they finally do. It is such a reality shift.

After Amy was born, our lives changed considerably. I realized, as all new parents do, how time consuming children can be. As much as my husband adored our little daughter, he also resented any time she demanded. He also discovered that children cannot be controlled just because you yell louder. The louder you yell, the louder they cry. Without the ability to win a battle, a warrior is lost, so new battles needed to be discovered. Sports were a great option since they called out all his competitiveness and aggression.

As a result, my husband started taking up sports at work. On Tuesday nights he had softball, on Wednesday it was volleyball and somewhere in there came basketball. Before long, a woman at work, who was on one or two of his sports teams, had asked him about becoming a member of the Ski Patrol at a mountain she worked at on weekends. Before I knew it, my daughter and I were home alone on weekends while my husband went away with his friend from the office to help our future. It was explained to me that this was the way in which, in the future, we could afford to ski as a family. No sacrifice on my part was too great if it was going to help the family. Rather than becoming closer, we were starting to live in different worlds. My needs for emotional support and stimulating conversation were demands he couldn't handle after a long day at work and that was the only time I saw him. Even then, that was only on the nights he didn't have sports.

My need for company on the weekend was seen as a selfish request that would hurt our family's future happiness. I saw first-hand how people who need to manipulate always find people willing to be manipulated. I thought this was love. I had so little experience I had no idea what it was supposed to look like, so everything he asked for seemed to cause me to learn to love just a little bit more. If I wasn't selfish, we would all be happy. It is like a magnetic attraction. As happens with so many women, I began to go into a survival mode. Anything that would keep us together was good. I wasn't totally oblivious, I knew there were problems here and they were not all mine. I was waiting for the day when he would wake up, when he would realize I was the best thing that ever happened to him, and we would talk about everything and anything. One thing I have always been is a perpetual optimist. I looked back over my life and saw that I had dreamed of getting out of the projects and I had, far out. I dreamed of becoming a nun and I had, and those years were a gift beyond measure. I had dreamed of becoming a social worker and I had. I had come to dream of being an airline stewardess and I did it. I lost the weight, I reviewed my French, and I got accepted. I made it through flight school and had lived quite a life. When I took the time to look over the journey I had traveled thus far, it seemed clear to me that God was walking right beside me. If I could dream it, I could make it happen. Now my dream was that this man I had chosen to marry, had fallen deeply in love with, and wanted to spend the rest of my life with, would realize our marriage was hurting. I wanted so much for the joy, the connection, the intimacy that I needed, to become present in this relationship. I wanted him to want me the way I wanted him.

I realized that all my other dreams were things I could accomplish with my own hard work, focus, and prayer. This dream entailed someone else. We can do anything if it is just our dream but this one meant needing him to dream my same dream. This was much more complicated and I was beginning to feel needy and desperate. Now, I recognize that stage as being in depression. I entered a period of very deep depression . For that moment, I was following in my mother's footsteps. Depression is the result of a belief in our powerlessness. The more powerless we feel, the more depressed we become. I was feeling more and more powerless to make John love me the way I wanted to be loved, and as a result, the depression got deeper and deeper.

There are so very many beliefs about depression and what it actually is. It is a fact that the serotonin in our system is out of balance but the how's and the why's vary, depending upon your beliefs. As someone who has been a holistic health practitioner for many years now, I have very strong beliefs that there is a spiritual foundation, and an emotional one, for any and all physical symptoms. Depression is a symptom. As someone who has been there, I know a great deal about it. I have seen it from all sides. I have seen people who have suffered from depression for years who have taken all forms of medication, legal and otherwise. Yet when I ask about their personal process, the choices they have made in their lives, and the choices they want to take in their lives, they have very little to offer. When I discuss risks, the risk of living rather than surviving, they often times become agitated, and go to a victim stance. As with many diseases, there are some who want change and will blindly follow to discover a way out, to find tools for health. There are also those who do not want to deal with change. As terrible as it may feel, there is a security in living what they know, what they have learned. For some, owning their power goes against every self-image, or even world view, that they hold and they don't choose to let them go. For those who do, but don't know where to begin, sometimes we need to act when we are not able to think things through. Act as if… Honestly, it becomes a reality. Unfortunately, at times when we need and want someone to help us do that we do not always have someone in our life to support us in that way. Depression may be a physical reality but that is not a justification for perpetuating it. Change your physicality by changing your perspective. It can be done but only if you are willing to take the risk of first changing your emotionality with or without help. Medication can be a useful and effective short-term intervention but it should only be used in conjunction with psychotherapeutic assistance, not as a substitute. I am all for whatever works.

After a year or two of going skiing without us, John finally invited us to come along on his ski weekends. I wanted to learn to love skiing and the long cold trips to Vermont every weekend. Somehow doing all the shopping, packing, and cooking in order to go away for a weekend and then minding my daughter while my husband skied with his friends was not enough to make me happy. I am sure having a wife that felt trapped and alone and a child who had needs didn't make him very happy either. Two folks who couldn't talk about anything and who each feared being abandoned didn't help our marriage at all. We both ended up feeling abandoned and we both definitely felt unloved. We wanted our marriage to work, we wanted forever, yet we had no idea how to do it and be happy at the same time.

One thing I did know that would make me happy was having another child. I had wanted my children about 10 months apart, Irish twins as they call them. We had no such luck. I ended up being on fertility drugs for a few years before I could get pregnant again. We would go to so many parties and it seemed as if every woman in the world was pregnant during those years. The heartache was awful. I had all this love and I wanted to share it with so many. At one point, I had prayed for 10 children and now I was struggling just to have two. John dealt with his pain in his way by keeping busy outside, while I was home with Amy. She could make me laugh. She was so adorable and huggable. I thanked God for her daily. I wanted to give her the world. Chutes and Ladders and so many other games were our past times. She always played them right while I always messed up. She lovingly taught me the game every time. I wanted her to have a brother or sister, a confidante and an ally, when she needed to be disciplined and didn't like us at the moment. I was so grateful for my brothers and sister and I wanted her to have the same gift.

Finally, I conceived my son Michael. He was such a love who brought such joy to my life. He, however, was very different from Amy. She slept through the night 3 days home from the hospital. Michael took 8 months to sleep through. It was another whole world. I had been told I could never get pregnant again and after three years of treatments and surgeries, we had him. I certainly didn't want to complain. Two children brought twice as much joy and twice as much frustration and exhaustion. At times I remember feeling as if I was living with leeches. Those babies would grab my genitals, my legs, and anything else they could get, and not let go until I figured out what they wanted or answered their questions. It is no wonder that so many women stop feeling sexy, independent, and creative at this stage. I thought that never again would I ever get to go to the bathroom alone.

One day I took a shower and had the kids locked in the bathroom with me. We had those child-safe plastic knobs on the doors that no parent can ever turn. When things seemed too quiet I looked out and the door was open. I panicked and looked around for the little ones. Michael was sitting on the kitchen counter, with the stove on, and watching the papers burn. He was feeding the fire. He had made a little camp fire for himself and was so excited. This one had more energy than I thought I could ever handle. I oftentimes prayed in thanksgiving for getting to a place at just the right moment. His creativity never ceased to amaze me. I hadn't realized being a mom was quite so challenging but I learned.

With just the kids around, I was so aware of being alone. I had no one to giggle with, and no one to cry with. At times I wished there was a girlfriend around because I had such a quick wit and there was always a funny comment to be made. (Since my divorce, I have made a point of always having a girlfriend in my life. They are not a luxury; they are an absolute necessity.) In so many relationships, especially addictive relationships, the controlling partner isolates their spouse. They forbid or discourage any connection to family or friends. Outsiders are seen as a threat to the control. In fact they are. A loved one, a special friend, can give you a perspective you have lost and that makes them a threat to the other's control.

During the day, John had work, which I envied. It seemed like heaven to me since there were adults there. Although I had no desire to leave the children all day, still I was home all alone. John's role was to bring home a paycheck and my role was to raise the children, keep the house clean, and make John's life problem free. If those didn't go right, I wasn't doing my job. We camped almost every weekend from Memorial Day until the end of September, and then we skied almost every weekend from Thanksgiving until Easter. It kept me busy and it got us out of the house. Things just went along as life does and, before you know it, many years had passed. We had some really good times and we had some not so good times, like anyone. From the outside everything looked good, two kids, two cars, a house, a riding lawnmower and a good job that paid well for John. We were holding each other back but from what, I had no idea, and I was too frightened to think about it, so we went on as usual.

When your dream includes only you, you have an amazing ability to adapt it as needed to reach your goal. When it involves another, however, whether a lover, spouse, friend, child or sibling, your ability to actualize it just as you envisioned it, can be greatly impacted by the other or others. It is your dream, not theirs. It contains your idiosyncrasies, not theirs. It is important to remember that it is your life, not theirs that you are most responsible for and to. If others chose to walk with you, it is a gift, but if they chose to leave or not be such an active partner any more, they have the right. If your dream isn't happening, what can you do to make it real? Change it in some way? Change your perception of it? With two people drowning in a dream that isn't working, it is important to see if one or both actually no longer fit this dream. Have the demands or the reality proven to be far more than one is willing to commit to? Was it the image that was wanted, but the reality and the cost of it too high? Our dreams are not us, they are not our life. They are only the venues in which we live our lives. It is so important to know the difference, whether it is a job, a location or a relationship. If it is healthy and we are ready, our dreams call us to grow in ways we never imagined. We become more than we ever thought possible. If the price is too high or we are not ready, we have a choice to grow quickly, or to postpone that level of growth. With free will, we even have the option of not growing at all. It is against nature but anything is possible when we are so frightened, and we are more willing to pay the price of stagnation and ego than of growth and ultimate freedom.

We truly tried and over the years we worked our way through a number of marriage therapists. After seeing several, I had learned a lot about therapy itself and thought about going back and getting a graduate degree. I needed something for myself, and I had loved studying. At about that time, also, and not coincidentally, I had the greatest low point in my life. For one brief moment, I can remember it as if it was yesterday, I was vacuuming in the corner around my plants, and I wondered how I would kill myself if I were to commit suicide. I took a quick second to explore each of my options and somehow realized that any way I did it, I would be leaving my children to be raised by someone else.

That realization shook me up more than anything had in years. It was a bolt that shook my reality on all levels. It was at that very moment that every ounce of energy that had been dying and/or barely surviving came fully alive for me. I decided right then and there, in that corner, that I would get my degree - either while we were together as a couple, or we got out of this marriage and I found a way to make it on my own. Never again was I going to just survive another day and never again was I going to have that level of depression. Never again would I allow myself to reach the depths I had been in until that moment. I was coming alive now, and I intended to stay that way. If being the perfect wife and mother meant having no dreams, no visions, and no life, I didn't want the job and I didn't want it for my children either. I did not want them depressed or anxiety racked. I came alive at that moment. I was tired of depression, of existing, and of waiting for God knows what. I was tired of searching for perfection. I wanted REAL for me and the kids. We deserved it. I was tired of asking John to tell me who he wanted me to be since, whenever I was me, he disapproved. He had told me, often, that others disapproved as well. At that moment, a new woman was born or perhaps the old one was back. Amazingly, as the years passed in my practice, I came to see it as a common theme, that when someone met their passion, for whatever reason, their life force jumped in at full speed and years of a pattern of depression just left. When you are in touch with your power and passion, when you see your abilities and act on them, you lose your belief in your powerlessness and the depression is relieved, naturally. Each of us comes to that place in our own way, if we let it.

John was willing to financially support school, as long as it didn't interfere with our family life in any way. That was his concession. I was seeing me coming alive and our marriage finally having a chance. He was seeing me come out from under and probably moving away. We each saw it all so differently. He was doing his best to help me be alive even though it terrified him. He truly wanted our marriage to work as well; we simply had two very radically different ideas about what a marriage was, and what it was supposed to look like. My husband believed that a woman gives up her life when she marries and becomes her husband's support system. Once she has children, she becomes the sole support of their every need as well. He told me once that I could not have a life until he and the children were gone. I gave up that right when I married. I had thought we were going to learn to share and to be each other's supports and encourage each other as we changed and grew. I realized that by living in that energy, that environment, I would die and long before any of them were ready to leave. It was as if I had discovered that part of me that disappeared on my wedding day. I felt I was whole again. I was so filled with passion and excitement and even anxiety about a new beginning. I knew I could do this. I knew windows and doors were opening. It was something I sensed. I so wanted John to get on board. I wanted him to be happy for me. Happy that I was feeling so excited again, about life, about every day, even as I was so completely grateful for this family I had helped create. Maybe, just maybe, this passion would fill us both and change this marriage we had to something we both enjoyed and looked forward to each day.

I wanted to come home and tell him what I learned, what I had discovered about me, about us. I wanted to debate topics; whether we agreed or disagreed didn't matter. I wanted an "us." What I discovered, however, was that John did not like my having any interests outside of the home. He never wanted school or any of my classes discussed in the house; he forbade it. If I were to take a class at night, dinner was to be made beforehand and the children fed and ready for bed before I left. Again, I figured I would give him time, time to see that I loved my family and him even more because I was so much more alive. I was so grateful for these beautiful healthy children and so grateful for this man I had chosen for my life partner. After a while, I realized John was just too frightened to want to ever know anything about my life away from him. He was too angry to think I would even want a life of my own. He considered it a betrayal of our vows. This time rather than going into depression, however, I confronted him on all the years he had had a life away from us, the sports, the weekends away, the women, and the booze. Things we were not a part of.

John had been right about something. My going to school would change things. It gave me a voice. It gave me back the power I had given away. It gave me back the ability to dream and to want things, to want a future that I loved. I so wanted him to be a part of all this. We had struggled financially as all young couples do. We had worked so hard to have these children when we were told we couldn't. We had achieved all our dreams together. Now, when we had the chance to give up struggle, to have two good incomes and travel with the kids, and also as a couple, when we had the chance to really live the good life, to teach those handicapped kids to ski, to get that ski house John had always wanted, and to make new dreams, I wanted it. I wanted the couple to be all it could be. I wanted us to be the couple we had dreamed about years ago. I was so ready and I so wanted him to want it.

I loved so fully at that point, that I was able to forgive the past - to let it go - the women, the lonely nights and weekends, and all the rest. If only we could begin again, with a new vision, and a new understanding of us. Throughout graduate school we tried. John was so aware I had changed and for him, change is bad. I was so aware I needed his support and his encouragement. I kept asking for it and he kept insisting that letting me go to school was enough support. He didn't have to be a part of it. My heart went out to him. The world he had tried to create was changing. He couldn't see that this new world I was trying to create had more joy, more fluidity, and more laughter. Control, obedience, and predictability were still of adamant importance to him. We had grown so far apart in so many ways. He loved his skiing, golf, Budweiser, and a few good buddies to hang out with after sports. He wanted a predictable life with a few good friends. I wanted to live life every day, open to new experiences as they presented themselves, to change whenever it was needed. I wanted to meet all kinds of different people and have a wide variety of life choices. I could never go back to trying to fit into the box John wanted. I wanted to discover a way in which we could each have our needs met while we appreciated and accepted the differences. I wanted John to be a part of this, of my life. I wanted us to stay together but I could also see this was John's choice. He could be a part of it or not. He could try to adapt, accept, and to love. He needed to decide if there was room in our marriage for me. Now, it was his time to choose.

Throughout our marriage I had been told by so many people that I was the powerful one in our relationship. I never saw it. John was the one dictating the schedules. He was the one who came and went. He was the one who said we could or could not go here or there. I was the one who struggled to be good enough. Only at this point did I see what they were talking about. I adapted, I loved, and I grew. John lived in his fear and in his rage. It was so sad to see. This man I had adored, this man I had given my life to, was so filled with fears that they would not allow him to change, they had him stuck. I wanted to bring him with me but he couldn't let go of the old ways, even when they failed.

Even with all these therapists, and some honest effort on our part to come to mutual understandings and expectations, we both saw the insanity in continuing. One man asked to see me alone, and proceeded to ask me why on earth I stayed with this guy since it was clear he was a waste; he was never going to grow up and never wanted to. Another therapist who had recently divorced his wife and married his secretary took the opposite approach. After seeing me for weeks in so much pain and my husband in so much frustration, one morning, after I had been in graduate school awhile and had discovered meditation and relaxation tapes, decided I must be on drugs since my affect was so different and suggested that perhaps that may be a major factor in our difficulties. There were others, but with all the help, and all the effort, I think we both just got too tired. It was clear, that after 15 years of trying, the marriage was not going to make it. He could not make room for me in his life and in our marriage and I couldn't go back.

I filed for divorce and I believe that in some ways we were both completely relieved and yet heartbroken. We had wanted it to work yet what it required wasn't necessarily something we had to give. I truly believe that at times there are just people who are meant to be friends, for a short time, but who have no idea how male/female friendships work, so they marry. I have seen it so often. It is sad. I believe John and I really did come to love each other. We saw the goodness in each other and, when we could allow ourselves to be undefended, we really did enjoy one another. Unfortunately, that became more and more rare. We both had parts of our personalities that blended well. We just wanted such totally different things in our marriage and in our lives. Staying together would have brought so much more heartache, and the resultant physical disorders, and our children would have had to live in a house that was rapidly dis-integrating. I couldn't allow that to happen to any of us. I guess I really was the strong one.

Over the years, I have developed an immense respect for mar-riage, not the duration at all costs type, but the kind that supports and displays the love, commitment, and mutuality of two people who have chosen to fall in love and stay there. I honestly believe we are all capable of staying in love if we choose. Loving is the developed art of seeing the value in another. Falling in love and staying there is the result of a choice to perpetuate an emotional response for someone you have committed your life to. It is a choice to avoid competition, and winning against one another, and to hold this one up as your lover for life. It means being willing to put them in a special light, seeing all of who they are, and still choos-ing to put the emphasis on their goodness and their blessings and not maintaining a list of their shortcomings and who owes who, etc. It gives hope to those of us who need to have that value and hope validated.

Our marriage had had some good times. It gave us two gor-geous children. We had achieved all the dreams we had had for our lives, except for the kind of marriage we had dreamed about. Over time with someone, you get to see more clearly what their perspec-tive is, more so than what they say. Ours were just too totally differ-ent. At one point, before my schooling began, I realized that all of my dreams for the past few years had been for my husband and my children. They were about what I wanted for them; what I wanted them to want. I really hadn't had a dream of my own in a long time. Even I hadn't made room in my life for me. Things needed to change or I literally believed I would die. It was then, really, that I began to understand that I had doing what I least wanted to do – I had been surviving.

I realized I needed to begin to dream again, for me, and it had to include my children. They were the greatest joy in the world for me. I had learned to love in ways I had never known existed because of them. Even with the experience of living with little creatures clawing at my body and actually sitting on the floor crying, hoping, and praying that I would live until the day when I would have an opportunity to go to the bathroom by myself, I couldn't imagine my life without them. We were now going to start again and in a whole new way. I was opening the doors and the windows in our lives. My kids were going to have the new found freedom I had discovered and then claimed. They were going to have the freedom to give up perfection and try self-expression, new experiences, and even failing at new things. My heart broke for John, for he deserved all this too, it just terrified him too much to risk trying, to risk letting go of the illusion of control.

# Chapter Eight
## Divorce

*Allowing a dream to die is a painful experience.*
*But it leaves room for the next dream to come.*

FILING FOR DIVORCE WAS SUCH AN AWFUL experience. I can understand why so many try to put it off. No matter what the reasons for the divorce are, it isn't just the marriage that ends. It is also all the dreams, all the hopes, all the illusions of what the perfect life was supposed to look like, and the illusion that you had it or at least were close. It is letting go of all the dreams you had for years, before and during your marriage. For many couples I have worked with, and with individuals, as well, it is not so much their partner that they are grieving, or even that they miss, since the relationship was usually dead long before the divorce took place. They discover what they long for and miss is having someone to hold, someone to love, someone to dream with and cry with and laugh with, someone familiar. That is the hardest part of all. You thought you had it all, and could even kid yourself at times. Now there are no more lies, no more illusions. It is over. Now you are on your own. What happens from here on out, is all of your making. How you go through this divorce is all of your making as well. You may have little control over what your partner does or doesn't do, but you have total control over how you deal with it. If you are going to do victim, that is a choice. If you are going to fight 'till death, that is a choice. If you are going to have a game plan but leave it open as things progress, that is a choice as well. How you go through your divorce begins to define how you are going to live the rest of your life. It is a long and painful process no matter how "amicable" you agree to be. It can bring out the worst and the best in you so be prepared. For most folks, there is a total breaking down of all that you thought you held dear, all that you thought was important. This is a time of death, and in death we do total reevaluations.

I believe John and I did it in the hardest way possible. My husband stayed in the house. The lawyer said he could and so he did. He sometimes went to work on Monday morning and came home Thursday night. He sometimes came home Tuesday and he may even have come home on Monday, the same day. I never knew. What I knew is that I felt as if I was dying. It felt like a long, slow, painful death that would never end. At times I could see such humor in my life and at other times each breath was as far as I could see. I had chosen to be fully alive but it seemed that I needed to go through the death of the old person first. There was great joy and hope, at last, but also great pain. Thankfully, with women friends, I came to count on the joy.

I discovered there is an entire underground of single women that no one knows about unless you discover the signs. You cannot go through this stage without a sense of humor. Develop one now or find a friend who has one. We have this one movie theater near us in Hartford, CT, Cinema City. It has some movies that were in all the cinemas as well as artsy type films. The first movie every Sunday, the one I went to, was filled with Single woman all getting their small soda and small buttered popcorn. You could see them coming for forever. My girlfriend Diane and I would laugh at ourselves (EXTREMELY IMPORTANT) and then at them and our connection in all this. It all became so familiar. You could tell by the clothes they wore if the divorce was going well this week, or, if it was a bad divorce week. You could tell those who had started dating, sexy was coming back, and those who had given up. (This usually entailed a large refillable, buttered popcorn and a large Coke, NOT a diet coke.).

We always finished it off with an ice cream. Hey, give yourself a treat! We made this a routine because we needed one. My girlfriend Maureen and I bought season tickets to a playhouse for years. It forced us to take the time to get together to laugh and encourage each other forward. We went through divorces together, teen years with monsters and then teen years with saints. Like every parent, we loved it and applauded one another when a child passed that sophomore year. We came to see it as cruel that by the senior year, when you love them again, they leave. Why didn't they leave in sophomore year when you would have paid a limousine to take them away, anywhere?

Maureen is the woman I called, literally, nightly for that year when John lived there, or, didn't. Sometimes I sobbed as I told her my story of the day while she so lovingly listened. Sometimes I was so filled with passion and hope as I succeeded at something or began to see the light at the end of the tunnel that she would just laugh at me. Sometimes I couldn't even talk and just wanted to hear all about her life since mine was so filled with pain I couldn't bear to bring it all up again. I just wanted to be transported to someone else's life for the moment, no matter what it entailed. It wasn't mine and that made it all OK. I couldn't really move on, since he was still there and yet it wasn't the same because he wasn't really there anymore. I think that is one of the more insane practices encouraged by lawyers. Whatever the legal benefits are, they should be dropped. Nothing is worth that torment, nothing. Once papers are filed, it is time to move on. There is so much pain it is ridiculous to intentionally add more or perpetuate it as it is.

Again, friends are an absolute necessity. Maureen was one of those angels who walked beside me when I most needed one. I don't know how I ever could have survived without her love, understanding, patience, and humor. When I felt I was dying, she was beginning to date. Now that was hysterical and the necessary salve we both needed to make our lives balanced. What a strange word that is, to describe that period in our lives, there wasn't any balance anywhere. In any event, dating after divorce is like no other time of dating. Thank God! Maureen's adventures and misadventures kept us in stitches. She needed to share them and I so desperately needed to hear them. I couldn't imagine ever dating again in my whole entire life but I so wanted to hear her stories. They were so comical and so poignant. She said so often, "He can stay over but he will never put clothes in my closet or dirty my toilet." For some reason that always made me laugh. I understood so fully what she meant. It was too painful to think of loving that totally again or of living with someone who could take it all away. Our homes began to symbolize so much of what we had survived and accomplished. We wanted our freedom. We didn't want anyone thinking they were in charge ever again and we didn't want anyone claiming what was ours, and yet, we so wanted to love again, or at least she did....

That period of divorce brings up everything to be looked at. All the fears from your earliest childhood memories seem to come back. Every fear of starvation, failure, struggle, and incompetence came flooding up. For me there was a terror of taking my children, who were 6 and 10, back to the projects, of never having a client in my future, of never being able to support my babies. I began to question my own competence as a therapist and as a mother. It became clear, and I have advised everyone I know, that it is very important to go into some type of therapy as you go through your divorce. Whatever you can afford, do it. What I discovered, is that with a girlfriend to support me, and a therapist to guide me, there wasn't anything I couldn't do. Finally, acknowledging that I can't do it alone made it all so much easier. That was a huge growth step for me. A Whitney Houston song says, "It's not right, but it's OK, I'm going to make it anyway", and that was pretty much what it came to for me. I had kept hoping my husband would wake up some morning and say, "Dottie, I love you, I want you back. I want to get to know who you have become. I want us to be a team." I wanted so much for it to work.

Finally, I could accept that after all this time, if it hadn't happened, it wouldn't and I needed to move on. After what seemed like years, but in fact was about a year, total, our divorce was finalized. I was free. I was so numb I just remember feeling mild relief, joy, and exhaustion. All I wanted to do was go home and sleep for about a month. It was over and I had survived it. I was not the woman who had filed. It had been a year of such tearing down and such rebuilding that I felt like an entirely different woman from the one who had walked in and filed papers so long ago. I believed the world was open to me. I just needed to get some strength back and then I would begin the rest of my life. Then I would create another dream. By now I knew that without a dream we merely survive. With a dream, we have something worth living for. It is a reflection of you, your aspirations, your gifts, and your truth. It shows you who you are now and who you are becoming.

My husband got friends to help him move out half of the furniture, half the dishes, half the glasses, half the silverware, and half the food in the freezer, and so on. We had gotten almost equal amounts of savings and equity, etc. Everything seemed to go in a pot, and we both walked away with about half. I got the house and a station wagon with over 100,000 miles; he got a lot of money and a brand new car. At least the kids could stay in the only home they knew. As soon as he and his friends started leaving with furniture, I realized I compulsively started reclaiming this house. I went into our bedroom and starting ripping wallpaper off the walls. I had that done so quickly it amazed me. All that adrenaline that had been building up in all those months of wanting to move on had come to a breaking point and was breaking out. I redecorated immediately in a style that was all my own with palm trees and planters and the bed kitty-corner. One thing I did, that very afternoon, was to call the phone company and tell them I wanted a phone in my bedroom immediately. With a totally different look and feel to my bedroom, which now had draped cloth on the tables, an informal canopy made from a broomstick suspended from the ceiling and sheets flowing around it, ferns and palm trees behind and around the bed, and a phone coming in that morning, I now had my room as my own. It was my haven and a symbol of what I wanted my life to be like, open, free, feminine, and mine.

That first year, my greatest therapy was in taking my house and my life back. I knocked down the wall (how symbolic) between the kitchen and dining room. I had someone put in a frame around it. The kitchen table was gone now so I installed a breakfast bar. With half my furniture gone, I could change lots of things around and have plenty of room. I had girlfriends in to give me ideas so I could pick and choose and add whatever I wanted. I went from a subdued traditional décor to island bright. My house became filled with hunter green and canary yellow; plants flourished everywhere. I had always wanted a study in the part of the basement that was unfinished. I went to the lumber yard and step by step I did it. I hired someone to help me put up a ceiling but I installed a window frame alone, a 20 foot windowsill, and so much more. It is amazing how much help is out there if you only go looking for it. I did and I found it. There is no limit if you reach out far enough. Although I could get heady at times with all I was accomplishing, I was still dealing with the reality that I was alone. I felt so wildly alive and yet so profoundly empty in some way.

Life, and nothing else, would ever be the same again. Every time I walked into the family room and saw that there was no furniture there, I felt as if someone had punched me in the stomach. I literally lost my breath. I forced myself to use my charge card and bought a 13 foot sectional sofa and tables. I could not live with that much pain ever again and I wouldn't. I needed life in every room. It was a glorious time and it was awful. I saw loud and clear that year, that we can easily have so called contradictory emotions flying around at high speed at any moment, each demanding full attention. Thankfully, girlfriends who found me to be obsessed with the house would drop by at times with sandwiches, bottles of wine, and lots of stories of the world I was missing out on. I loved their visits, but I also knew I needed to listen to my heart and my own needs. I needed to make this house, and my life, mine. I needed to get me and the kids settled in our home. It was so much lighter and freer. The changes, the completions, represented all that had gone on in our lives recently and the closure we were getting with it.

Although I had been devastated and heart-broken at the end of my marriage, I was ALIVE. My children were happier. They began to create more and more dreams for themselves starting with their dream bedrooms and their dream meals. Since I had so dramatically changed my room, they wanted to do the same. Things were freer and more alive and we all wanted our lives to reflect that. They were blossoming. Amy, who had been an anxious child with a twitch, lost the twitch within a week and became confident and very much preadolescent. It was so wonderful to see the kids were so relaxed, playful, silly, and creative. We had all started coming alive and we were contentedly happy and at peace. Mike wanted all his time at home. He didn't want the every other weekend away. Legally, I was forced to have him go. The pain his departure caused in me on those weekends was physical as well as emotional and spiritual. As a result, I worked harder to make our time at home together everything I wanted for him and Amy. Divorce is so hard and the worst part is seeing the babies suffer. They deserve none of that pain yet they get so much. As I saw it, the alternative was to stay in the marriage and have them in pain all the time and with me dead before too long. The only choice was to go forward, following my new dreams for them and me.

I had been so clear about healthy meals and home-made jams, jelly, breads, tomato sauce, and so on. Now things were so different and we all loved it. They loved tacos, pasta, and pizza – so who cared? Our menu became very limited but we sure enjoyed the meals. Life was so very different for us. Within six months, I had a six-month waiting list for my practice and yet I was always home after 6:00p.m. for family dinner which one of the kids cooked. Friday nights, however, were different. We all took that night off, with a celebration of pizza, paper plates, and soda in front of the TV with a rented movie on our new VCR. We all ate together. That was of immense importance to me, to be able to maintain my family as a solid structure. During the week, I did the dishes and they did homework. The practice I had been asked to join was growing beautifully and I was developing friendships that were everything I could have wanted.

I had been frightened about starting a private practice. I still felt so wounded, so unaware, so green at this professional-life thing. What I came to realize quickly, was that the humor I had developed in my early family life, the ability to love unconditionally I developed in religious life, the ability to distance from problems I learned in the airlines, combined with all the painful and joyous experiences of my marriage and divorce, made me exactly what so many patients needed. I hadn't just read about life and studied psychology, I had lived it. I truly understood their pain, joys, and confusions, I had lived them. The specifics may have been different but the experiences, and the emotions were all the same. I had the best qualifications a therapist could have, and I had chosen life over survival and lived the journey. As the patients kept coming and making referrals to friends and coworkers, I came to believe in my gifts more and more. I certainly came to love this new ministry. It was a very old dream being lived in a very new way.

As the kids got a bit older and could stay up later, at 8:00pm they got to watch TV for one hour and I made popcorn while we were all sitting together on that big sectional. Let me tell you, if I never see 90210 ever again in my whole entire life I will still survive quite nicely. With all the pros and cons about television, and, I had restricted it when they were younger, I discovered that some kids will share a lot more if the TV is on than at other times. Although there was a lot of talking at the dinner table, this continued it. I watched shows I thought were ludicrous but I discovered so much about their classes, their friends, their teachers, and their failures while we were watching television. Somehow it made it safer for them to share. With the kids being my sole focus now, I could really watch and learn so much from them, just in the watching. If you just watch, without comment or judgment, you can see how your children view the world, how they adapt or don't adapt when things go wrong, and what they do when they hurt. Few children can verbalize those things but they are so readily available if you only take the time to watch.

They are such a gift to us. Don't you just want to look at some of the beautiful things you own and appreciate their beauty? It is no different with our children. It is a huge mistake to think you know them because you were close when they were five. Hopefully, they are changing and growing every year and if you don't pay attention you will never really know this precious gift you have been given because he or she will be transformed so many times over before they are grown.

Our life certainly was not perfect after the divorce but my children were more relaxed, we were all happier and freer, and we were starting to develop a life with new routines, new schedules, and a whole new outlook on life. We were beginning again. By the time Christmas came and we got our first real live tree, we were all moving forward. We certainly felt the absence of my husband that first Christmas which made it somewhat bittersweet. At the same time, however, we were developing new traditions for our family and each of us was putting our ideas and wants into the pile so that we all had a say, and each became a part of the dream for us and for the future. My marriage was over, my divorce was over, and now we would begin again. The three of us formed a team and we all had important roles to play. Amy became the protective big sister. Mike brought heart and vulnerability to the family. I loved them both unconditionally while I worked to create the stability and comfort I wanted them to have. Mike asked that we eat by candle light since, he said, we ate slower then and spent more time as a family. Amy complained she couldn't see what she was eating and she had friends to call right after dinner and so she couldn't take long. Our life as a family was as full and as normal as I could have hoped... New dreams were being lived. There were dreams for my family, dreams for my life, and dreams for peace and joy. They were all unfolding every day and they were dreams that were shared...

# Chapter Nine
## Post-Divorce

*When freedom and self-discovery create the backdrop.*
*You get to create the dream without limits.*

WHEN I WAS FIRST DIVORCED, I THOUGHT it would be a stabilizing point for my children if we stayed in the house they had been in since birth. So for five years we stayed in the small town they were born in and in the only home they knew. Having done so much work on it, we made it ours; we each made changes to it that filled our needs. I had never seen myself working full-time when they were young so it was all still a major adjustment for me. At times, I was still so angry because this wasn't how it was supposed to be. I was supposed to be married and with my husband who was supposed to love me and only me. I had so much to deal with emotionally and physically in maintaining the family, the house, and my practice, I decided it would be best for all of us if I just focused all my energies on those things. I would wait years before dating. Besides, I still had too many things I needed to look at in regards to what I did to contribute to the ending of my marriage. I wanted to make sure that if I ever considered marrying again, which I doubted I would, that I would not make the same mistakes again.

I was so aware that the cookie incident in the first year of my marriage was really the beginning, or perhaps I should say the formalizing, of how it was going to be. The standard questions of "What if" came up often in those days. What if I had said, "No, I will not return these. We are both working, we are both contributing here and I want these"? What if I had stood up and said, "I am an equal partner here and this conversation is ridiculous."? What if I had taken my power back the next time it happened? What if I had been stronger? What if ....... It is a common consequence of divorce. We never really get an answer because it is very rarely that simple, but we sure do try.

My children said to me one day, "Mom, how come you never cried when you and daddy got divorced?" I was stunned. I thought all I did for those first few years was cry. I cried in the car coming home from work because no one would be there to love me and ask me how my day went, how I felt, or what my dreams or fears were. I cried doing the dishes because there was no one in the parlor I could yell to and share an anecdote from my day with. I cried because the lawn mower had only three wheels and I couldn't afford to get it fixed, so I practically carried it when I mowed the lawn. I cried almost every night in bed because there was no one there to hold me and love me and tell me it was going to be OK. I cried because I wanted my children to have a father who treated them with gentleness and love and an appreciation of who they were. I cried because never again would it be the same, never again would there be a chance for that illusion that we could make it work and, at times, I just cried. I would hear so often how it is harder on the one who files or it is harder on the one who gets served papers. It is amazing how everyone (usually those who have never been through something) have so many opinions. I know my story, but I cannot imagine it is easy on anyone, whatever the circumstances.

As impossible as it seems, eventually the crying slows down, and even stops. I found it is essential to bring new things in to fill the void as well as new traditions and rituals. Activities need to change so that you really do begin to create a new life for yourself. At some point, you need to acknowledge that your past is gone and it is time to move on. It is time for a dream. For every one of us, that timing is different. Every one of us has different responsibilities and different abilities in letting go. Any ability, however, gets developed, just like a muscle, by using it. I started walking with a girlfriend, getting in shape, feeling better about myself, and feeling better physically. Going to the movies on weekends when my kids were with their father became a routine. I started going out to lunch on workdays with partners in the practice. I may have only ordered a small salad but I was out. I was developing friendships and I was developing me as a woman. I knew how to be a wife and a mother and now I was learning how to be a woman. It is amazing the things we never learned. So many of us became so associated with our roles that we never bother to figure out how we fit into them or how much of us we express in those roles. We usually let others define for us how they should be done and we do it.

I discovered that I am really quite an "outrageous" person even though it all seemed so normal to me. I learned that I am actually very powerful and vivacious. Qualities I never would have considered claiming. By going out to lunch and interacting with others and by simply allowing myself to follow some of my dreams, I discovered, in using others as mirrors, that I have a style all my own. As simplistic as that may seem, I never knew that. Peter, a dear friend in the practice, would say on occasion, when I wore a new outfit, "Wow, you look like you just walked off the cover of a magazine." I knew, incredulously, that he meant it. It wasn't flattery; it was real. I don't know if he will ever realize the impact of that honesty and that statement. What a gift of love. I hadn't thought of myself as anything but a mom for so long that these "little" statements threw me into a whole new level of self-awareness. I was actually becoming a woman and not just a working mom.

I spent the first five years after my divorce, fixing up the house and gradually buying the things we needed and wanted. My first "major" purchase after the divorce had been an above ground pool in the backyard. The kids and I had talked about it for years but John hated the idea. He wanted to save money for his ski house some day. I bought a large oval pool and had a small deck put on with a gate. It was about the smartest move I could have made at the time. It helped change the entire feel of our house. I swam several laps every morning at 6:00a.m. from May to October and felt so free and so alive. If you haven't noticed, those two feelings are immensely important to me. The kids played in it all day and had their friends over. The joy and excitement it brought to the house made it everything I had always wanted it to be. I couldn't care less about the noise or the amount of water or juice or cookies we used up. That was no longer a concern at all. I was in charge of the finances now and we would always have enough for friends.

I had about one-third of the income I had had when I was married, yet I felt richer than I had ever been in my life. Comparatively speaking, it may not have been much money but it was mine. I could and would spend it any way I chose. The next thing I bought at that stage was a VCR. We "couldn't afford one" when I was married but I bought one soon after the divorce and did it ever add to our family time… The kids wanted to rent the same movies over and over and it became a family joke. When they were gone, and it was a rainy or snowy weekend, I was in heaven with a pile of movies at my side. It only took a few simple purchases and our family and our home were transformed. During the summer, the kids decided a week-long soccer camp was an absolute necessity if their futures were going to be successful. This was going to make them great high school stars and help them win full scholarships to college. Mike had no idea what college or a scholarship was but someone had given them quite a pep-talk. In the beginning they went to day camp. They then decided sleep over was so much better for their futures. Since it was twice the money, I couldn't see it until my girlfriend told me that if they went to camp, I had one week off. When she followed with the idea that perhaps we could take trips to the Caribbean each year while they were away, it was clinched. We all got a vacation each summer and I simply took shorter lunches and saw a few more clients earlier in the morning after the kids left for school.

Things got settled at home and the rituals and styles had solidly changed. I had my season tickets to the theater with Maureen, did Sunday afternoon movies with Diane when the kids were with their dad, had lunch with my partners at work, and spoke to friends on the phone in my bedroom in the evening. Finally, I had a life. I never thought I would get there, but I woke up one day and there it was. Now that my present was set, I had an entire future to plan and to dream about. My practice had continued to grow and even become highly successful. I had stopped being shocked by that and was simply accepting that when you find where you belong, it works. My spiritual life had become such a major part of my life that I was exploring it in so many ways and in every area of my life.

In my practice, my patients were thrilled with the work and felt that they were getting to places in weeks that had taken many months with other therapists. A common statement I heard was that they, when referring friends to me, would say, "You cannot BS Dottie. She sees right through you and calls it as she sees it. She is great." I loved it and knew it was true. After a while, however, I felt a piece was missing but I didn't know what. On someone's recommendation, I went to see a woman, a psychic, and asked her what I should do to make the practice feel whole to me. This was my first venture into the world of the psychic realm. It was all so weird and yet felt so right in some strange way and so strangely familiar.

Here I was, an Irish Catholic, an ex-nun even, going to talk to a Protestant woman who was channeling an 18th century Scotsman about my life and my spiritual beliefs. Life never ceases to unfold in the strangest of ways. This woman told me my gift was in my hands. I had no idea what she meant, since although I had done so much work around the house, I just felt we would starve if I was meant to be a carpenter. She told me I needed to begin with acupressure and I would then be led the rest of the way. I had never heard of acupressure so it was a stretch to begin with. Not coincidentally, a man in the outer room asked me how it went and I told him about acupressure. He told me he goes for a treatment regularly and he gave me the practitioner's name.

The rest of my life was beginning to be defined and I had no idea what was to come. I had taken the first step to the rest of my life, down a road I had never heard of or thought about. When I called Sam McClellan in Massachusetts and told him why I was calling, he accepted it all as perfectly normal stuff. I was the only one still shocked, a little bewildered, and greatly curious. Sam had a program starting up the following week in which he taught his normally year long program in the summer which would be meeting daily for six weeks. For whatever reason, I decided to join. I had long ago given up the concept of coincidence and felt that too many things had come together for this to happen; I just had to go there. Everything external was supporting it. I was looking at life so differently now, on so many levels. Trust and taking a leap were the orders of the day. I knew it was a big leap although I didn't understand the details. I just knew it was only the beginning of so many more changes to come from the ripple effect of this course and boy was I right. We do know things and need to trust that knowing even when we can't label it. It is all inside; we just need to let it out.

Sam was a great teacher. We had a small group that got close quickly as they usually do in that type of setting. I learned about things I had only sensed before but never explored. The meridians, the inner energy flows of the body, were fascinating and overlapping them with the emotional strata made it absolutely intriguing for me. I love working with psychodynamics from any angle. People are such fascinating and complex individuals. To learn about balancing their emotional responses through physical manipulation was so exciting. All this came so naturally to me. At home, I got a college student to mind the kids for the summer during the day while they swam in the pool with friends, and we still had our dinners together. The kids were at their dad's some of the weekends and at camp for two others. I would miss the Caribbean this year but this was too good and too life-transforming to miss. As a result, I worked 12 hour days on Saturday and Sunday to make sure the money kept coming in to pay the bills. In our field, summers are usually much slower since so many folks go away to their second homes, so it all worked out well. The couple of days in the office kept the clients happy and the bills paid.

When I completed this program, Sam referred me to his mentor, the creator of Jin Shin Do. I then studied with her and became certified in her modality of treatment as well. This was all getting to be so exciting. My whole world view was changing. I was beginning to see so clearly the intimate relationship between the body and the mind. What a phenomenal awareness that was. Although I have always loved studying psychodynamics, now the study of it through the body fascinated me beyond words. I felt, again, as if I was coming alive. I was entering a whole new world, a whole new reality that was on a level so much deeper than any I had known before. It was at this point that the importance of spirituality and the acknowledgment of the spiritual realm moved into my work.

Spirituality took on a whole new meaning. That "something" that had been missing was now found, and found in a way I never would have anticipated.

In the office, it all began with one woman, one Irish Catholic woman. She had come in to see me with Fibromyalgia as her presenting problem. About 90% of all patients with this disorder are women. It can be a very painful experience. It was an entirely different experience having patients present with physical challenges rather than psychological issues. It called for major adjustments to my self-image and my approach to my work. I had no mentors to follow in this transformation. I see now what a gift that woman was to me and what a gift we were for each other. She was a school psychologist who had been put on pain medication by her doctor. It caused her to feel groggy, so she started to become depressed. As a result, he put her on an antidepressant. That made her anxious because she couldn't work at top level. She was holistic in orientation as well and all this was against her beliefs. By the time she came to see me, her medications had been changed to an antidepressant/anti-anxiety combination with the pain medication as well. When she came to see me, she was hardly able to walk and was holding the wall to support herself. She came because she had heard that I was doing holistic work. We worked for a few weeks taking her history and making some mild changes.

Because by now I was fully aware that all physical disease has an emotional trigger, I asked her what was going on at the time of onset. She told me her daughter was leaving for junior year abroad and she was terrified that she wouldn't be there to protect her if she needed her. Once she found out she was going, the pain began, but she had never connected the two. When we looked at the connections and could begin to change her perspective on her daughter's decision, real progress was being made in the treatment. It was around this time that we took a giant step, for the both of us.

One day, she was on the treatment table in the office and I had my hands on two meridian points, waiting for a response. I knew it would be around fear and sadness simply by the points I was touching. She started crying quite a bit and after looking at her to make sure she was OK, I just happened to look at the wall behind her. When I did, I saw a picture, as if I was watching a TV screen. In this picture, there was a little girl, around 4, sitting on a bed with a chenille bedspread, drawing rainbows. For God knows what reason, I asked her why she was drawing rainbows, as if it is normal to see active pictures on a plain wall, and my patient said because they made her feel better. I, the solid intelligent therapist, almost panicked. What on earth was going on??? I saw a picture, thinking I must be crazy or having a breakdown and didn't know it, and for some reason I ask a question out loud and my patient answered with a logical response???????? Nowhere in grad school were we trained for this. After a moment of shock, or terror, I went with this whole thing. I was lost on this one. When I looked around this picture I could tell she was in an attic because of the eves. When I asked her why she was in the attic, she said that was her bedroom and that all her older sisters had gone out to play and they didn't want her hanging around because she was just a baby. She told me she went to the attic and closed the door so that she didn't hear mommy and daddy fighting again. While all this was going on, and I continued with my treatment somehow, she started feeling better and better. She saw both the sadness and fear that were also in her life now around the decision her daughter made. We had gone back in time to the first time she felt the connection of these two emotions, remembered it, and healed the wound that had still existed on an emotional/energetic level. As a result, her disorder left, never to return. She gradually came off all medications, and within a short period of time she began coming every two weeks, then every three, once a month, and finally just for "maintenance."

She was in a great place. I still questioned if I was crazy or if I was making this all up. I needed to talk to someone fast. NONE of this made sense or settled in easily for me. I saw it. I knew what had happened, and I saw the "miracle" after all but none of it made sense. I really was being asked to let go, again, of a method of understanding. I was being called to another reality in understanding, in seeing, in believing, and in doing my life not just my work. The co-creation was continuing. When I shared all this with Barbara, a trusted friend from the practice, she treated it all as a normal occurrence. She reminded me that my gifts were in my hands, and that I had so many, many gifts. She had such unconditional faith in my work and that has remained to this day. That kind of acceptance, and that faith in me, carried me through quite a lot. When these visions, or movies, became a pattern, she started referring her patients to me who were stuck in their psychotherapy. I would work with them for a few sessions, "seeing" where the problem began in their childhood, etc. and then sent them back to her. Others started referring to me also. It seemed to me that nothing in my life was as it had been. Once I became acclimated, I loved it yet I was walking totally in faith, not knowing where I was going or how I would get there. I was living a dream of faith, freedom, and discovery, and with unlimited fulfillment. It was everything I had ever wanted and so much more. I knew then that I simply needed to trust my inner knowing. I would know what was right for me and I would know where to go, from inside. I felt so blessed. Life is such a gift and, to think, at one point I thought of throwing it away. Thank you God!

Once I had settled some after all this occurred, I needed to know what this was all about. Why me? Why now? I went to see a very elderly woman, Ada, who was very much the old grandmother

I never had. She had great psychic skills and talked often to the angels, and to me, about my children and myself. She had said to me once that I needed to leave my marriage if I was going to live. She had also said that I was not able to grow spiritually in that marriage because I was so squelched in any attempt to create an "I." In order for spiritual growth to take place, we need freedom and joy and play in our life, if only internally. We need to be in a place without chains or limit because that is the energy of the soul. That is how we are meant to live. With my new life, I had all that and so I was now free to discover and grow. Why me? Because it was a gift as old as Solomon and a gift that was now mine. What gifts do you possess? Which require that you make changes in your life? Are you willing?

Now, in this post-divorce period, in this process of forming a new life for myself, as a woman and as an individual, I created a prayer, which I said daily, for years. "Lord, help me prepare, in whatever way I need, for the next step on the journey. Support me in doing what it is I have come here to do." It is really the prayer of my life. Whatever it is I came into this world to accomplish, I pray that I achieve it in the best way I can, whatever that entails. The next stage was moving along with excitement, and a little apprehension, to places I never could have dreamed.

Again, we can create a general dream, for freedom, for joy, and for life but have absolutely no idea about the specifics of what that is going to look like. The more specific the dream, the more the chance you will achieve it and the more able you are to work with it. I believe we create a dream and as large as it seems to us, we are really only looking through a 10" lens. The Holy Spirit has panoramic vision. We think we are reaching for the stars but someone greater knows there is so much more out there that we cannot even comprehend and then makes it all available to us. We put our best effort into this, and the rest is co-created. We never walk alone. It is our responsibility to dream the dreams and then, together, watch it all unfold. As each of my dreams had been lived, I can now see so clearly that they were built on one another.

Each time I created a dream, it asked so much of me in terms of personal growth, in terms of spiritual development, faith, trust, and a willingness to recognize that all things are possible. Whether it was having the two children I was told I could not have, having a successful career when I had been left scared and alone after my divorce, transforming my house by learning how to use all those tools I had been so frightened of, or learning how to help others heal, all those things were dreams, and they all asked so much of me. Without the dreams of them, none of it would have been possible. Each called me to develop tools I hadn't experienced before. Each required me to reach out further, to become more than I was previously. Each demanded I live more in the truth of who I was, more than I had ever done before. Each was the reason for me becoming me. Those dreams, each one of them, became my mentors, my guides, and my gifts. Always, I remember Tom telling me of my courage, when I felt none, and yet now knowing that without it, without the willingness to risk, I never would have had the ability or developed the focus needed to make it all come to life. We have so much within us that is so important to discover. Dreams are what call us forward to do just that. They give us life, ourselves, and a deeper connection to God who makes it all come together.

How often have you realized that you never could have done something alone? How often have you realized that it was no accident or coincidence that you met someone or found something, that it was placed right in front of you? You only had to open up to seeing it. For me that is the gift and the joy of co-creation. It is a reality that takes place, all day and all night, if we allow it. Even more, how often have you realized you "should" have been some place when, in fact, if you had, you may have died or missed one of the greatest opportunities of your life? For me, always, there is a reason, usually beyond our immediate comprehension but nonetheless, a reason.

# Chapter Ten
## Single Mom and Single Woman

*Sometimes two dreams can coexist.*

WHEN I WAS DIVORCED, AMY WAS IN the fifth grade. She and Mike went to the same school and were in the same car pool. Once she entered high school, our whole lives became so much more complicated. We lived out in a rural/suburb area. It was in that setting that we had created a lifestyle that worked for all of us. As the kids grew, however, it was working less and less.

Once it was time for high school, Amy had to commute for one half-hour each way. That meant I got up very early, made lunches for the kids, and took Amy's car pool into the city where I worked and where she went to school. I would then come back out to Granby where we lived and then take Mike in his car pool to the next town over for elementary school. Then I went back to the city to work. This started to seem somewhat insane rather quickly. What finally made it intolerable was when Amy decided to do track. She would say, "I have a meet tonight, Mom, could you pick me up at school at 10:30?" I hated to leave my Michael alone even though it was a safe neighborhood. He was in the fifth grade by now and I was working hard on not thinking of him as my baby, but it was taking time. It can be so hard for a mother to let go of the last one when you know this is it. I needed to be fair to him but it was such a struggle. I also didn't want to limit Amy's ability to be as involved in school as she chose.

After more than one meet going way over time, and the bus coming in closer to 12:00 midnight while I sat in the high school parking lot waiting, I decided we needed to move closer to Amy's high school and to my work. I realized I would sit in my car torn about going back to get Mike, who wanted to sleep in my bed if I was going out, in order to feel safe, and yet wanting to stay and be there for Amy. Life had become nice and almost easy. I wanted it to stay that way for awhile but it was clear time was up and change was coming in again. I could feel the balance, the ease, collapsing as another major decision needed to made, alone. It was a very difficult period. I was so aware of being a single mom at those times. It is such a difficult process when you try to raise children alone. Because I hadn't dated since my divorce, I had never had that extra person to ask to go get Amy or stay with Mike. We lived so far out and I had no girlfriends in the area. The grieving of the loss of a dream can come back again and again at the most unexpected of times. As you heal, however, the pain is lessened and it comes less frequently.

It is at those times, however, when we are most vulnerable. It was at those moments that I most felt like a failure as a mom, that my loneliness and the loss of my husband most hurt. It was at those times also when we would go to the Spaghetti Dinners and the concerts that followed that I would see my ex with his new wife looking so together, knowing that they had just spent a long weekend at one of their timeshares skiing or playing golf. I was thinking of how many patients I needed to call when I got home, after I checked to see if I needed to make cookies for the bake sale or do something else that they absolutely needed for tomorrow.

As overwhelming as all that is, the idea of not having our children can be paralyzing and it is a fear that occurs when you least expect it. The common response when an ex remarries, in a theoretical discussion, is "Thank God. Maybe now he will get off my back." or "Thank God, maybe now they will move far away." The reality is so much different when it actually happens. It is more common to feel devastated, abandoned, furious, and betrayed. At that time, many, as I did, also throw in another emotion. Because my dream for my children had been to have a two-parent family, the terror that went through me when my ex remarried was that perhaps the kids would want to leave and go live with their dad. Maybe they would want that two-parent family as much as I had wanted it for them. Also, John and his wife had a lot more money than I did and could take the kids on ski trips all over the country or the world if they chose. I couldn't. What if my children chose to leave? Could I live through that? It was another fear to put in the pile when I was feeling weakened already.

Being vulnerable and frightened by another move momentarily took me away from how far I had grown. It was amazing. I went from feeling so spiritually alive, so aware of other realities, so solid and together to the times when I could let that comfort slip and I would then get caught up in the details of living. In adjusting to all this, I also came to see that overwhelmed was one emotion I needed help with. It was old, from the days in my father's house, and now it was back. Thankfully, I knew it was the feeling that made me aware it was passed time to call a girlfriend. We each have a particular emotion that precipitates our falling apart. Whatever that feeling is, when it comes up, it is an absolute necessity to reach out. At the first sensation of that emotion, CALL NOW. It is saying to you that you have been giving way too much and receiving way too little. When that emotion sneaks in, stop immediately. Self-care is as important, if not more so, than taking care of others. I mean that without reservation. If you do not take care of yourself, you have nothing left to give. It was at those times when a girlfriend would say, "We are doing dinner tomorrow. Let the kids order pizza; they will be in heaven. If you aren't around, they will eat it on the floor in front of television and feel real cool and think they are putting something over on you. Give them the illusion of winning one, they deserve it." That one evening of tears, shared inadequacies, laughter, and friendship would transform my world and bring it back to normal. Somehow nothing seemed impossible after those evenings. A renewed perspective can change your life in one evening. If you don't reach out instantly, you spiral downhill real fast. It can take a lot longer to get back and then you have a lot more catching up to do.

Having faith in yourself, in your ability to land on your feet, and to define how you want to do your life is based on reality. There is nothing that comes into your life that you can't handle. There may be things that you don't want to handle but there is nothing you can't handle. You must reach out for help when you need it. You will eliminate a problem quicker when you do, or, you can plan a strategy to deal with whatever is up at the moment. Once you know all this, on a cellular level, there isn't much that can throw you for long. Some use their power to intimidate, some use it to manipulate, some refuse to acknowledge it, and some use it passive aggressively, but we all have it. What you do with yours is your choice, so why not use it to your advantage? Use it to support where you want to go and do what you want to do. If you need help, ask for it - don't go to victim. If you don't understand, ask -don't go to victim. If you need a mentor, go get one - don't go to victim. Victimhood is a mentality for those filled with self-hatred and a lack of self-awareness. It is an illusion that justifies, in your mind, not living in your truth or going where you need to go, but, it is never the truth.

Owning that power, owning my ability to now make large decisions for us as a family, I was now ready to take us to a better place. Once I realized we needed to move to make life easier for all of us, and I had the emotional support I needed, I started things rolling. A house search began. It took months to sell our home which was a necessary first step so that I could afford to buy another one. In the meantime, I looked through the paper every Sunday to see what was up for sale in the town where Amy went to school and where Mike would soon go also. It was also the town where I worked. The ease it offered seemed so extraordinarily easy. I was ready... A new dream was beginning, again.

This move symbolized so much for me. It wasn't just moving from a rural/suburban area to the city. It wasn't even just moving to a town where I could have a town bus drive the kids. It was moving the kids to a place that was 3,000 sq. ft instead of 1600 and where we would go to school, work, and socialize all in the same town. If I wanted to see a movie, it was 5 minutes away. If I wanted to go to a play, it was 5 minute away. If they needed something at the store for those last minute school projects, it was a few blocks away. If Amy had a track meet, she called me when the bus got to the high school. It was few blocks away and it felt sooo much better. This was city living and I am a city girl. For me, it was so clear on some level, that in this move, I was going from a single mom to a single woman. I didn't know how or when; it was just something I sensed. We moved from a 6 room home to a 10 room house. The difference was immense. I felt as if I was moving into a dream house in a dream world. It wasn't just a bigger house, it was another whole level of living, one I never thought I could achieve, especially alone. Another self-created limit was released.......

I was so elated and yet so terrified. I find that to be a common experience for me in watching my dreams come true. I become elated because at one point it was only a hope, then it became a dream and, finally, it became a reality. Nelson Mandela has a wonderful saying that basically describes how we are actually most terrified of being powerful, not powerless. It is something I truly believe. Feeling powerless can make us feel saddened or depressed but feeling immensely powerful can be so very frightening. If I am

powerful enough to make all my dreams come true, then I sure better know exactly what I want before I put it out there. Also, what if
I dream of something I am not capable of doing? I could make a fool
out of myself. My intellectual belief on that one is if you can dream
it, by the time you reach it, you have grown into it. If not, get a
mentor fast and catch on. You can do it!!!!!!! Your dreams really do
call you to move forward to the next natural step in the progression
of your life. That is why, without a dream, people stagnate. There is
nothing calling them forward. Nothing is stimulating their passion
and asking them to become more, to do more, and to be more. We
need that and we need it to come from within. The dream is the
thing that helps us actualize the newest expression of who we are to
become. It is a gift we give ourselves.

Once the basics were done, the appliances unloaded, and the
beds made, etc., it was time for the full unpacking. I do hate clutter
and disorganization. I went to the store and bought 13 mini blinds
and 6 pairs of window shutters. I had taken two days off from work
to get settled and the kids were in school so there were no inter-
ruptions. I was on a natural high. I was all over that house. Between
installing shutters downstairs, mini blinds in all the bedrooms and
upstairs bathrooms, and unpacking, I was a whirlwind. I also had
the cable man in since the kids thought a fate worse than death had
appeared  - no television. That guy ended up staying most of the
day since the place needed so much work with cable everywhere
along the house and roof from the last owner and I wanted the TV
hookup on two other floors as well. Since he was here already, I figured I'd get the future plans started so I wouldn't need to call them
out again for an additional service charge. This man watched me
running around all day. Finally, just before he was ready to leave he
asked me if I danced. I had no idea where that came from and said I
hadn't in about 20 years but once upon a time I loved it. He asked
me out for the next night to go dancing. He figured with all that

energy I must be athletic or a dancer. He said he couldn't imagine the energy since I was exhausting him just watching the things I had done. It is still amazing that men get flabbergasted when a woman can do so many manual things around a house. If you do not have the money to hire someone and you do not have a man in your life, your choice is either to go without what you want or learn to do it yourself. That's easy. I will learn. There are always sales people ready to teach you and guide you if you go to the right stores. These home supply places have done a great service for single women everywhere. I built a room in the other house, this was kids' play.

In any event, after not dating since I married my husband 20 years before, I was terrified of dating. I had no idea how to act, or how to dance anymore. The kids were at their dad's for the weekend so they didn't see me changing outfits for hours as if I was 16. I was too fat, too old, etc. etc. This would be a hilarious comedy routine if I wasn't on the verge of collapsing into tears at any moment. When the kids were home, I stayed in; when they were at their dad's every other weekend, I went out with friends. This was the first time it was a male friend, however, and that made it all so different. We went out to two different dance clubs Friday and Saturday since each was popular on different nights. I had never dated much to begin with so this was all really quite an adventure. I called Maureen often asking for help and hints. The new dating thing after divorce is such a hassle. Whoever would have expected to be in that situation again? How are we supposed to know what to do? Last time I was an ex-nun in cultural shock, so much so that I never really dated. This time I just felt out of the loop. If you are not talking about kids the way you do with girlfriends what on earth do you talk about? My girlfriends were all psychotherapists or at least close to the field. What do you say to someone whose work is so different? Also, women are so different from men and this proved it...

I knew on some level I would begin dating with this move, I just never expected it to be so soon. I was having a great time once the terror and self-consciousness wore off. After two weeks, he decided to introduce me to some of his friends. To say the least, it was a very eclectic group. I met Hannah who had been divorced for a while. She was a Jewish girl from Cleveland who was dating a man, James, from Dominica. There was another couple, Betsy and Isaac. She had been in the Peace Corp in Liberia where she met Isaac who was from one of the villages she worked in. They later married and came to the U.S. Sabas was from Honduras and he worked with Isaac at a local psychiatric hospital. They were like an extended family since no one had family in the area.

As time went on, it just so happened that we celebrated all the Jewish holidays at Hannah's house and all the Christian holidays at mine. I loved the diversity and I especially loved my children being so much a part of it. I really believe that bigotry and prejudice all come from ignorance. I had very little difficulty with Mike not liking one of the kids because they were younger and thus dumb (there can be a huge gap between 10 and 6 when one wants to watch sports and the other wants cartoons) but I would have been really dismayed if it had been faith or race based. I believed, and still do, that we all won in that situation. We used to call ourselves a family by choice since it wasn't by blood. On a Sunday, I may have put in a roast beef for the three of us, only then to have Hannah call and say she would love to get together. She would bring over a big salad and her two kids. She would call Isaac and Betsy and they may bring a lamb along with their two kids. Someone would call Sabas and he would bring wine. (He was single so our expectations were different.) Mike and the guys may go outside and play soccer, or downstairs to play pool or ping-pong while the women cooked. Amy would be on the phone with friends. I really felt so full with such an extended family. I love having a community around me. I believe we all need alone time to remember who we truly are and to stay in touch with our dreams and our lives but we need community to be whole. I had found it all thanks to Roy, the cable man. We became good friends but only that. He was anther angel sent to help me come alive and begin the movement from single mom to single woman with a life of her own.

Hannah was continuously trying to fix me up with so many different people but there wasn't a one I was the least bit interested in. Somehow, in a strict Catholic upbringing, I had thought that once you consented to date someone you were saying that they were a potential life partner. I guess we took it all so seriously back then. Sin was always lurking around ready to jump at the slightest provocation. It never crossed my mind that you simply dated someone to get to know who they were as a person or simply to have an escort at a particular function. In my past, if you dated someone once, you were a couple and that was that. This was a whole new world and one I found very difficult to adjust to. So much so, that I stopped going out with anyone. I just couldn't figure it out and I never thought I would be confronted with it again so I had never thought I had to learn it all. Isn't it amazing how naive we can be in some areas when we are so wise in others? Life is such an amazing adventure.

With the kids and I developing a routine, having a wonderful extended family, a blessing of intimate, healing friendships, and a successful practice, I was being pulled to grow even more professionally and personally. I had studied acupressure, become certified in Jin Shin Do, and was ready for more. I spent four years studying spiritual healing through energy work with Barbara Brennan in Long Island. Five weeks a year, students from all over the world came together to study and to learn about energy fields, health, guardian angels, and all the unlimited power that exists in each one of us. It was an experience that changed my life. I came alive in ways I had never known were possible. I developed skills to see energy around the human body. I came to see so fully the connection between the mind, body and soul in holistic health. I discovered gifts in High Sense Perception that took me to levels of understanding that surpassed anything I had ever imagined.

During one of my healings, I opened my eyes momentarily and briefly saw a woman in white standing next to the student who was giving me a healing. Her presence felt wonderful. When the healing finished, I looked around the room for her but no one in the room was wearing all white. When I asked him about her, he laughed and said that that was one of my guides and she wanted to help him help me. It took a while to let that reality sink in. There was actually a guide walking with me, there was actually someone who could be seen, AND I saw her...

That period of wonderment continued as I began to see inside the body, to see tumors, pregnancies, and clots. It was all so much to take in yet I continued. The "intelligent" part of me questioned if this was all from the power of suggestion or from fantasy or imagination. I needed proof or scientific evidence. Something to prove this was all real; that I wasn't making this all up. I would try to get others to tell me what they saw before I would say what I saw. I needed to know that someone else saw it also and the same way I did. I needed things affirmed for quite a while before I was able to acknowledge that these were way too many coincidences, with too many others seeing what I saw, for me to keep my doubt. I got rid of doubt but not shock. I was awestruck.

Along with all of this, I came to understand myself, my behavior, my fears, and my personal journey in such a way that self-love was allowed to flourish. I had never been so alive, so aware, and so grateful for my journey. It is amazing how much there is to learn. No wonder we are never done... I had moved into having a practice in holistic health by incorporating psychotherapy, acupressure, Spiritual Healing, Jin Shin Do, Hypnotherapy, Reiki, Breath Work, and a few other techniques, all of which I had become certified in, into one eclectic approach. About this time, with a new home, a new approach to my work, the beginning of my post-divorce dating period underway, and my daughter now in high school, it seemed only logical that my work location should change as well.

Our field can be so intense that I needed someone to laugh with when we were both free; someone to help put things in perspective and/or run things by. Two other women, Barbara and Lee, joined me and we could divide expenses in thirds and really come out ahead. When you are ready the good Lord provides. We found a beautiful office, a newly refurbished building that was so extremely elegant. We had truly come up in the world. Within three months we had increased our income by an extra 40%. I was ecstatic and the two of them were in shock. I had done it! We took a risk and made it work.

I was, and still am, a licensed Marriage and Family therapist and a licensed individual therapist yet the patients who were coming to me changed. I had made immense steps in my own personal process both with the office move and with the new field of study. I continued getting people who were presenting with physical illness and who wanted alternative health care. These people wanted energy work or they knew that there were emotional issues beneath their illness and they wanted answers and resolution. Everything was changing. It never ceases to amaze me that, in this field, the clients change as you change. For me, that is one of the many affirmations in believing in God. To me, it affirms that we are not alone. There are no coincidences. Things happen with such synchronicity that it all has to be so much greater than us alone. We are all so interconnected. The change in one creates change in the others. Think of how important it is, and the effect we have, when we choose to stay in integrity. Think of the impact when we stay in truth, when we follow our heart. We are powerful beyond measure, every one of us. We are powerful enough to draw into our lives all those things that can support our dreams or destroy them, based on our expectations. Now, THAT is power. I was discovering all of this as my practice was changing. It certainly makes life choices so much more significant. It is so important to think and act consciously. We all have that ability to walk around half-present but think of the impact if we don't.... All these realizations certainly changed my life. I had always thought of myself as a global citizen but now I saw it even more so and with so much more of an effect.

I started teaching in graduate school because I love to teach and it was a way to expand my practice. Amy was getting ready for college and more money was needed. My life was moving on, and that was always a surprise, since in so many ways it just seemed to go one day at a time and I hadn't noticed that many days go by. My little girl now needed to look at colleges. When do they get so big? My dream of a family, of closeness between the three of us had happened. We were truly all in this together. We had gone through the stages were I was old and an embarrassment, where Mike was dumb and so immature, and now Amy was leaving. Her second year of high school and claiming "adulthood" had been quite a year but we all survived. Ironically, when I cherished them again, by senior year, it was time to leave. I wanted her flopping on my bed, after an evening out, giving me details, to go on forever. I wanted to be a part of her romances so I could hold her and soothe her when needed and laugh with her when it was good. I wanted to be a part of her exams so I could make her a late night snack if she was studying late.

Instead, I paid some organization at school to deliver care packages to her during exam times. That was as close as I could get with her in Georgetown and me in Hartford.

I knew it was time to let go, I just didn't have to do it joyfully. Our weekly (or more) calls were usually to make Mom feel good. When Amy really needed me, she came home. During a broken romance, Mom still held her, cherished her, and hurt with her. We bought her evening gowns together for those special events. Letting her go was easier once I knew I would still have her. We developed a ritual where I would take her down and get her settled in her new room each Fall. That first year leaving her in the dorm was exciting but so bittersweet. As each year went by, it was a little easier, a little more natural. I was letting go and I knew she would still hold on but in a different way. She wasn't my little girl anymore but she would always be my daughter. In the years to come, our relationship would change but always so sweetly. God is good and my dream for my family, as it was, was fulfilled. We truly did love each other and want each other.

Every child has their own personality and Amy's was certainly passionate. No one can ever accuse her of being laid back. I loved it. Now it was in Washington DC and our house was totally different. I wanted to hold onto Mike tighter since I knew his turn was next, yet I wanted to let him have as much freedom as a freshman in high school could have. It is amazing the dilemmas we can create when we try to do it all consciously. I also knew it was time to start developing a different relationship with him. He was becoming a man and getting his license was top on his priority list. I wanted to get to know him first, as a young man, not my baby, before I let him go too. That meant making the changes in me and in my perception of him as he was adjusting to high school while I wanted to protect him from all the mean upperclassmen. I desperately needed to focus some of my energy elsewhere. It would be best for both of us.

The best way to bring balance into all of this was for me to "get a life" as my kids would say. For me then, this meant continuing to have my friends in at home. It is always about balance and working things out. Mike got a phone in his room, and I went out on occasion after dinner to a movie theater just down the road and left him home alone, happy and feeling like a man in his castle. How, when, and where to make changes was the constant framework I used to deal with when creating "a life." What the universe sends in and how we deal with it all has a lot to do with our journeys as well. Boy, do we all bring in different stories….. If you say, I want change, change most certainly comes in. If you say I would like to meet a man (or woman) you better put some definitions down and make it specific…You get what you ask for, so know what you want. I learned the importance of details in the strangest and most unforeseen way.

# Chapter Eleven
## Adventures From Afar

*Dreams and wishes can bring the unforeseen.*
*Be ready and keep laughing.*

AT ABOUT THE TIME I HAD PUT out there that I wanted to start dating again, my girlfriends and I had all sat down and made lists of the qualities we wanted in a man. We hadn't had much luck before so this seemed a logical next step. We had never tried it so perhaps this was the step we had missed. It is amazing how women can be so educated, so self-aware, and so powerful, and yet so ill-prepared for dating. It is as if we are walking into another realm, one of unknown realities never before seen by adult women. I know some men feel the same way. Whether it is the experience of divorce, our dedication to our children, or our involvement in running our businesses, SOMETHING makes us unprepared for this stage. I had tried it 5 years after my divorce, learned a lot, made some naive mistakes, and then hid again. So many men seem to have the ability to stay out there. Women however can always justify running away from it all to kids or work. Each time then, seems like the first. Intellectually, we learn a lot from our experiences, but in terms of application, it is like the first time on ice skates all over again.

My friend Isaac, originally from Liberia, West Africa came to the USA because of Betsy but many of his countrymen came because of a seven year civil war in Liberia in which hundreds of thousands had been killed, tortured, or displaced. To keep their connection to their homeland alive and present, every year all the members of his particular tribe who now lived in, or east of, Chicago would have a reunion. This particular year, Isaac was the host so it was to be held in Hartford and he and Betsy were in charge of all the details. Because I had such a large house with two empty bedrooms, he had asked if I would put up a minister or two with their wives for the week long reunion since money was more limited for them. I was very open to the idea since I love to meet people from other cultures. There is always so much to learn. I had learned in my travels that the more we travel, the more we see other places, and the more we meet other peoples, the more we realize that we are all in this together. We come to see that each country, each group of people, has something to offer. There are so many things of value elsewhere. How can you not appreciate what so many others have? Values, life styles, and cultures may vary some but you can see the wonder in everything on this planet if you look. You can also begin to appreciate, more than ever, living in the USA. Most people have no idea what luxury exists in the USA, what gifts exist here, or what benefits and freedom you have simply by being a US citizen. Travel and exposure to other worlds can teach you so much about other cultures and remind you that in the USA, your greatest limitation is yourself and your ability to dream.

As a result, every time he asked if so and so could stay, I would say yes. Within a few days, he would say plans have changed. This went on a number of times when I finally said, just let it happen and trust the Holy Spirit. Well, when the day came and I walked into his house, blond and all dressed in black, there was a very large, very dark man sitting in the dining room all dressed in white. The contrast was a sight to see. There were people sitting all around him. Some were on the floor, others on chairs, some standing, etc. I walked into the room and just stared at him as if to say, "Where have you been?" He just stared back at me as if we had been intimate friends for forever. The other folks turned to see what was going on between us. When I was able, I went to Isaac, mesmerized and said, "Who on earth is that man?" You know that feeling you get sometimes, when you know you know someone, yet it is impossible??? That was the feeling. I knew I knew him, I knew I had met him before, yet this man had never been in the states before and I had never been to Liberia, yet I knew I knew him. Isaac said, "That is your house guest. He is a presidential candidate for Liberia. The civil war is ending, God willing, and he is one of the candidates running for president. He is in this country campaigning." I was frightened. I had no idea what all this meant but I knew, on a cellular level, that things in my life were about to change. I had no idea how, or in what way. I just knew things were about to change. I wanted to run yet I wanted to stay. I was scared and excited, willing and yet reluctant to take that next step, whatever it was. It was as physical an experience as it was spiritual and emotional… and so it began.

After dinner, trusting Isaac fully, I took my house guest home. This wasn't a minister and his wife, this was a presidential candidate. I had no idea where to go from here. Once home, we had a drink and relaxed. We talked about life, politics, my work, his work as an MD, a veterinarian, and a man from a country at war. I learned so much about another culture, another world. It was a week filled with such interesting conversations, such a life beyond anything I had ever experienced, thankfully, for some of it. Isaac and mutual friends would visit every evening as we all discussed the civil war, the upcoming elections, the U.S. role in it all, and the activities of the warlords. It was intriguing, compelling, and a world away. When Dak had to leave to go to the United Nations at the end of the week, I was disappointed and missed the interesting qualities of the past week. When he called and asked if he could return for a brief period to pursue some political interests in Connecticut, I was more than willing. I was being exposed to a way of life and a side of politics I hadn't experienced before. The more I came to know this man, between his trips to DC and to the UN, the more intrigued I became. My friends and I laughed about the lists we had all made on the qualities we wanted in a man.

I had listed INTELLIGENCE since I found so many men threatened by my role and education as a psychotherapist. Some were threatened by my owing my own successful business since they assumed I made so much more than they and thus thought them less somehow, so I wanted SUCCESSFUL. I am a powerful woman so I wrote POWERFUL so he wouldn't be threatened by that either. I wanted a peer and a partner. Finally, I listed AVAILABLE as well. He appeared to be all of these things. If this is what I said I wanted, was it really? If this was what I said I wanted, now that it was here, what was I going to do about it? It is so much easier to want something you don't have to deal with. To actually get what you say you want, to know you have the power to manifest it, forces you to deal with your words. The expression *put your money where your mouth is* came to mind.

This meant Mike and I needed a way to incorporate Dak's visits into our life as a family. Mike was the center of my life but I needed an adult relationship. It seemed as if nothing in my life came with directions or a role model to follow. It was continuously a dance of seeking balance. Sometimes it worked and sometimes it didn't. I had come to see myself as a helpmate and a partner. I had come to expect as much from him as I gave. This was all so brand new for me. It made being in a relationship with him that much more exciting and new. Since he gave so much in terms of support and encouragement, I willingly gave as much in return. We had so many cultural differences to work through that it took time to deal with each. He was a man and expected to be agreed with when he made a statement, or proclamation, as I would call it. To me, it was one of two adult opinions. We both needed to learn how to do this without making either one the bad guy. I would go to my feminist rhetoric and he would go to his "but I am the man" routine. When it was clearly pointed out that the greatest distinction was in the pants, and we both wore them, and he liked me in mine, he usually stopped in his tracks and would simply shake his head. I also learned that although he went to that defense, he did respect my opinions; this was just all new to him.

As a male physician in Africa, he was used to being viewed as being very close to God. I had written a thesis on Liberation Theology from a Feminist Perspective and he read it. I also wanted to be treated as someone who was close to God. Dak respected intelligence and power so it wasn't a big stretch. In public, I would be less forceful and he would be more observant. In terms of housework, when I worked and he was home, it made sense he would help out. He usually had the time and was willing to help. He needed time to be alone and so did I, without explanation. I felt as if I was always learning. This is what I had thought a relationship was like yet it was the first time I had ever had anything like this.

I came to care for him more and more as time passed. It was such a wonderful experience being with him. He treated me like royalty and expected the same. I was being given the opportunity to be with a truly powerful man and one who was not the least bit intimidated by me. It was glorious and hard. If he had lived up to my expectations, I needed to live up to my expectations as well and that was so much harder. Thankfully laughter was a large part of our life together when we were alone or with close friends. Having your dreams come true doesn't make life perfect, it only gives you the setting in which you do the rest of your growth.

At one point, after we had been together, he invited his children from Germany, Texas, and Liberia to come to meet me. Once they came, he told the girls to call me mother from that point forward and although they were only ten years younger than I, they were thrilled. We had all been speaking on the phone throughout this time so I felt I knew them well. They had already been turning to me for mothering or help with dream interpretations, etc. Once they saw us together, they laughed at our relationship and said that their father had never treated a woman in this way. They had never seen him so in love. They mentioned four women he had been involved with, or married to, over the years and stressed that I had all the best qualities of all four of them combined into my one personality. They were convinced that was why their father was so taken by me. It was like being hit with four women at one time and he was defenseless and in love. I was overwhelmed. I sat at my kitchen table listening to these girls plan the house I would live in once we moved to Liberia after the elections. They would stay with me when they came to visit since my house was so much more alive and joy filled. They had it all arranged. They planned my house boy, my servants, my car, etc. They were trying to teach me how to allow the servants to wait on me since they were convinced that I would feel bad after watching them work all day and I would make them dinner and wait on them, thus, throwing the entire chain of command out the window. This was truly another whole world, one I didn't know if I could fit into.

When they started talking about his wife, who was not their mother and who they definitely didn't like, I was totally thrown. It was then that I learned that this man was from the Gola tribe, and they were allowed 5 wives. I had asked for available and I got it. Never again have I used that word. Single is the operative word here, not available. When I said I needed time to think since I had to deal with a lot in a short period of time, he called his wife who in turn called me back. She thought my reluctance to be quite funny. She was welcoming me into the family and looked forward to meeting me. I was finally getting in over my head. We never know where our limit is until we cross it. I was on the line. When it was suggested that Dak go to Ghana to participate in the peace talks, we both cried. We had no idea when we would see each other again. It was heartbreaking letting go but I knew I needed time and he needed to go where it would serve things best.

In our time together, Dak had met many of my friends and family. I met many of his tribe, and other tribes from Liberia as well as some of his children. Most importantly, I had experienced a relationship like nothing I had ever been in before. Dak honestly wanted me to be in my power at all times even though he had no idea what to do with a woman like me and I certainly had no idea how to relate to a man like him. We had an argument in the kitchen one evening when we were both exhausted and the tensions were high. I had to leave to pick up Mike from a school event and Dak was cleaning up after dinner. We had been arguing over whether or not I was too emotional for an intelligent woman or whether or not he was too repressed for an intelligent man. (You know we were exhausted if this was what we found to argue about.) He told me quite strongly that I wore my heart on my sleeve and that was a sign of weakness and I told him he was so repressed from sitting on his emotions he was getting a fat ass. It is amazing how we could argue, and even in the midst of it, see how ridiculous we were being. As soon as those words came out of my mouth I gasped in shock and then burst into laughter. I couldn't believe what I said. I was usually so well controlled. We both laughed at the craziness of the argument as well as the phrases we were using. Once we stopped laughing, the argument began again. This was all entirely brand new for me. Somehow, as powerful and big as he was, he had taught me to fight and stand in my place when I disagreed with anything, even him, and I was.

That period of my life was such a God send. I had finally become comfortable, and unapologetic, about being powerful and having ideas and opinions. I had a man in my life who wanted my full participation. What an experience and what an adjustment. I learned I loved it that way, but still, half the time, I wanted to kick him. When you think about it, we say we want an equal partner, but at times don't you think we want an "almost equal" partner, who will acquiesce once the pearls of wisdom flow from our mouths? It was quite an experience for the both of us and one I would never give back for a minute. When he left for the peace talks, and then took what appeared to be a quick trip to Monrovia, Liberia to see his family, things would change.

There had been a price on his head by some warriors and Dak was forced to go into hiding. He was moved every couple weeks to a different house and would tell me my presence was keeping him alive through regular phone calls from wherever he was. It was only later, once he was safe, that I could accept that his way of life was more than I could, or wanted, to take on. He had been a gift to me, as I was to him, as he told me so often, yet it was time to focus again on my family, my job, and my future. It was time for him to look at moving on after the war ended and seeing where he would go from there. I could not risk losing my children as I traveled to another part of the globe. It seemed that this gift, this dream, was now coming to an end.

Life was moving forward and another adventure in dating had taught me more than I had expected, and a lot more than I thought possible. I had had a dream about dating, about finding a man who could love me as me, and about bringing in someone with a whole list of qualifications. I had had another dream come true which had been more than my list had asked for in many ways. I learned to be more specific and to recognize that I could create whatever I expected and wanted. I had also had the wonderful joy of having a man in my life who could laugh at me, and with me, when we were arguing, who could see the craziness that comes about when our egos come into play. He could also hold me, and affirm me, saying just the right thing. Until the day I die, each time I go into a feeling of powerlessness, defeat, or overwhelm, I will hear him say with all his solidity and power, "Dorothy, remember who you are." I saw so clearly that I needed to create a dream in my mind, focus on it and my ability, to make it happen and then just let it occur. As Linda Ronstadt says, "The impossible takes a little time." God willing, we have a lot of that.

Nobody can take our dreams away. Only we have the ability to throw them away or to replace them with something others deem to be more "practical" or more "realistic." As far as I am concerned, "realistic" is totally dependent upon your view of reality. Was it "realistic" to think that a girl from an Irish Catholic family in the projects of Boston, who was terrified of going crazy as a child, was going to become a nun, an international airline stewardess, a wife, mother, single mother, highly successful psychotherapist in private practice, an adjunct graduate faculty member, the founder of an institute of learning and then, when conditions seemed right, bring in a wonderful, powerful African politician? It all depends on your reality. Your reality can be as large or as small, as expanded or as limited, as you choose. What is your choice? I did not say what are you comfortable with... I said what is your choice? Which do you choose? What view of reality do you want for you at this point in your life?

If you can dream it, you can live it. The real question is, the only question is, are you willing to pay the price? I can assure you the price is very rarely about money. The real price is in your willingness to grow, to let go of preconceived notions of what is possible, or impossible and, most importantly, your willingness to take risks. Playing it safe does not allow for growth, it does not feed the need to become so much more than you ever imagined. Each time you take a risk, you discover another level of freedom, another understanding of the power of choice. Each time you risk, you take another step in the process of your unfolding, of becoming who you are beneath all the fears and self-imposed limitations. Most excitingly, each time you take a risk, you make it easier and easier to dream..... and..... to dream without limits.

# Chapter Twelve

## A New Dream

*If you pay attention, life guides you in making your dreams
happen. If you pay attention and consent, you grow.*

MY LIFE LOOKED AND FELT NOTHING LIKE I ever could have anticipated.
Every dream I ever had was only one segment, one small piece of
the puzzle. All those dreams, all the pieces to the puzzle that had
been dreamed and then created, were creating a picture that was
beyond my wildest dreams. We know so little when we innocently
create one small piece, even when it feels so huge to us. I truly
could not have created this life, this journey, alone. It has been so
synchronistic, so in alignment with who I am, who I never realized
I was. I believe completely, that someone else also had a hand in
it. Perhaps it was all those I loved who had passed already, perhaps
those guardian angels I brought along with me, and perhaps the
Holy Spirit, who I was told would always be with me. In just a few
short years, I had gone through so many changes, so much growth,
and so much exposure that nothing could ever be the same again. I
felt blessed beyond words.

With Dak gone, Mike and I had our life back to something re-
sembling normal again. Mike was getting ready to get his license to
drive and was exploring the idea of what college to attend. I was
aware I would need to look at making additional money for another college education. I had been teaching classes in Self-Healing
through the Energy Field for quite a while. I offered a series of
6 classes every two months in the conference room of our office.
Although new people came each time, there was a core group of
people who came back every time, repeating the course. When I

asked why, they said there was just so much more they wanted to learn and each time I did something slightly different. I finally took a risk and in prayer asked if this was meant to be a much more formalized program with a more structured curriculum. On the chance that it was, I put flyers in my waiting room just to see the response before deciding to go bigger with it, in terms of advertising. If so, that might be the way I made money for Mike's college tuition. It also was the opportunity to teach what I loved. I relished the idea of teaching so many others what I had learned at various schools, from my own experience, and through my personal process. It seemed like too big a dream to fathom but this was me; on some level I knew I could do it. It is really something how we can see others as leaders, as mentors, or as important or powerful teachers but not be able to own those qualities ourselves. Because it felt so right, so exciting inside (Don't all dreams when you first allow yourself to experience them?), I decided to pursue it. If it was meant to be, and I put all my effort into it, I believed it would happen. I trust Spirit completely.

My friend, and long term business partner, Barbara, had taken a leave and gone to Sedona, Arizona for an extended stay to look at where she wanted to go with her life. She invited me to visit for a week and so I did. Mike was going away for a week and I thought I would use the time for reflection and play. On the plane it became very clear to me that this trip was not about play. Again, it was not something I knew, just something I sensed. I just knew this trip was going to be life changing in some way but I had no idea how. I said a prayer that if I needed to grow through something in order to be ready to teach, then I was willing to do what was needed. If this school was where I needed to go for the next step in my process, then I wanted to be ready for it. I wanted to get rid of whatever blocks may impede the success of the program. I had decided that 10 was the operative number, but when I left, only 7 people had signed up for the school. With all the rent I would need to pay for the weekends the class would take place, the supplies and handouts, etc. I would need to purchase, and all the time involved, I needed to make a certain amount to make it worth my while. I believed if the school was going slowly because I wasn't ready, then any growth I may undertake on this trip would expedite the process and open the energy for the school to take shape.

I became ill only a short while out of Phoenix, where I had landed. Barb had picked me up and we had gone to lunch. I told her something didn't feel right but I didn't know what exactly. What followed were a few days of real illness and extreme discomfort on every level, emotionally, spiritually, and physically. After a horrific nightmare, in which Mike was being hurt and I could do nothing to help him, to get to him, I was awake shaking and sobbing all night. That nightmare touched me in every cell of my body. It brought up fears I could not have imagined having, at a level where I honestly didn't know if I could survive. It shattered my sense of self and of creation. How could anyone be so cruel and could I ever survive my son, my child, being so wounded and so frightened without being able to get to him? I could feel things inside of me blowing apart energetically. I had no idea what was happening to me and it was terrifying, as terrifying as that nightmare. Once daylight came, Barbara took me to see a healer in town. She worked with me for three days. I came to understand what the nightmare was about, why it occurred in Sedona, and why in Barbara's house across the street from the vortex next to her. I needed to have my entire energetic system loosened up and that did it. Fear and vulnerability make us very open, very pliable, and very susceptible to transformation. Someone on a higher level saw what I needed, I had consented and the growth took place. I was asked if I wanted to come to Sedona, I was given the opportunity on the plane to accept the invitation for growth, and I had consented. For me, this was another example that we never walk alone and that always, always, it is a co-creation when we allow it. Thankfully, not all steps in growth are that horrific, but always they are fruitful. It truly depends upon what we need at the time. There are no coincidences.

I came to understand as well, that in preparation for this school to open and to succeed, I needed to own my ability as a leader as well as a healer. I had become very caught up in my discovery of my High Sense Perception skills. The developing ability to see things on the energetic level, to perceive things at a level far deeper than I had ever anticipated, and to "know" things, had become so fascinating and exhilarating, that professionally I was no longer looking at growing. Professionally, I had become stuck. It was time to grow again.

This trip made it clear both by working with the healer and in conversations with Barbara, as well as in meditation, that what was needed now, if the school was to succeed at all, was a willingness on my part to own the role of leader and guide to all those who came to me. This really required a major change in my self-image. I was going to claim my healership, my ability to identify and heal the cause of dis-ease in someone and not just temporarily alleviate the symptoms, to the world. I was doing it on such a level that I was telling others not only was I a healer, but, I was such a good healer that I was qualified to train others to do this work. I was contemplating taking a somewhat controversial modality of health care, claiming it as a modality I supported, thoroughly, and then becoming a leader in it. That was a huge leap in ego definition for me. I was really putting myself out there and that felt like a huge leap off a big cliff.

The day I had made all these realizations and began to work on owning my power, my leadership, and my business ability, I called

Connecticut to check the status of the school. That very day, the enrollment went from 7 to 32. Calls had been coming in over the answering machine and applications had come in by mail. It was another one of those affirmations that says there is no such thing as a coincidence. I believe that so fully. I did what I needed to do to spiritually be made ready for this endeavor and now Spirit was doing the rest. Everything has an impact on everything else. We just do not always opt to see that, perhaps out of fear, or, out of resistance to our own power. The reality, however, is shown to me so often I have to accept it as fact, or, work very hard to not see what is in front of me. I actually find it all reassuring since, for me, it is a reminder, again, that we do not walk alone. There is a power so much greater than ourselves at work and we are all working together.

Returning to Connecticut now meant that I had to make up handouts, define a curriculum, do advertising, find a location that was large enough and that allowed various lunch locations. I also needed to hire an employee. Now that was another major shift in self-image. It made this sound like a real business, and I was no longer solely a therapist in private practice. I was becoming a multifaceted business woman as well. It was all one more step in my personal growth, in owning my healership, in public, and in claiming my leadership abilities. I had no idea what I was getting into but who does when they start a new adventure? It never comes out exactly as you envisioned. If you are blessed, it comes out being so much more.

I spent two weeks looking around at all the options for a location. If I was going to do this, I wanted to do it right, with style. I also wanted it near a variety of eating places, if possible, so the students could have a wide choice for lunch and/or dinner. Because this type of training would be so intense and so personal, I believed 18-20 was the maximum number of students who should be in each class. Consequently, it now meant I would need to do this program twice, on consecutive weekends. I had decided it would meet one weekend every two months, giving me two weekends on and six off. That gave them time to assimilate what they learned, to practice any techniques I taught, and to read what was required, as well as to grow into the next step along their journey. It also gave me, I thought, time for myself and to catch up.

I now needed to develop a curriculum. Now that I was really going for it, there was so much I wanted to teach. I had wondered if I would have enough information to share if I really went this big. Now that I was doing it, I wondered what to leave out. I had really done it. I had reached far and the students were waiting. It really caused me to stop for reflection. Everything in my life, repeatedly, kept telling me, JUST DREAM IT. I did, and here it was, dream after dream after dream. Why had I and so many others kept thinking this was impossible? What was it that made us think that only a few blessed souls, or rich souls, who could make their dreams come true but that the rest of us were destined for so little? What belief had we all been taught that had said "don't dream," "don't reach," or, "don't get too big for your britches" as my dad always said? I was getting smaller in my britches and loving it and at the same time so many, many dreams had come true. I believed so many others would also, once I was able to dream them. It seemed I had found the secret: dream it, focus on it, clarify it, put it out there, and then jump. Taking the risks necessary was the key and then you just pay the price needed. If it is worth it to you, it is yours. Asking for help, for mentoring, and for support is so necessary. Professionals, experts in this field or that, or simply people with experience, can be all the tools you need, depending upon your dream. Going for it made it happen. I had come to see that all my dreams came true once I committed to them, and, once I refused to give up. I had learned, also, that the finished project rarely looks the way we first envisioned it. Flexibility, openness, adaptability, humor, and faith are required. Taking things too seriously can cause a massive down fall. Life is short and it is truly the journey not the outcome that makes it worth the trip and that applies to our dreams as well.

Becoming a Spiritual Healer, becoming someone who would intimately work with others to allow them to see their soul, to see those parts of themselves that perhaps they have spent their lives avoiding, required being able to do the same thing with yourself. As a result, I felt it was my responsibility to take my students to that place where they would undergo the process first. Along with my natural, and developed, gifts and skills for seeing people for who they truly are, below all the masks and defenses they present, I chose to utilize a methodology called Core Energetics which was simple and easy to understand, yet very profound. It would be one of the tools I used to bring them to that place in themselves where they could shine, where they would know their truth. I believed it would also work in helping them understand how they did or did not do relationship, with anyone and everyone.

For myself, I had learned, so clearly, that going it alone no longer worked for me and I did not desire to live my life in my will, forcing myself to get through things. I wanted to enjoy what I was doing and look forward to each day. I had proven enough to myself, I had nothing left to prove. I hadn't even integrated all that yet. When I had done the original planning, I didn't take into consideration all the time needed to correct homework, all the calls and e-mail from students with a thousand questions, as well as all the students who would want psychotherapy sessions after a really great, productive weekend. As a result, I hired Barbara to assist in teaching the second freshman class.

Barbara's presence added a whole dimension to the school I hadn't anticipated. Our long term friendship had allowed and created a level of intimacy and mutual understanding that we just accepted as normal for us. For many of the students watching it, however, this level of trust and mutual respect and understanding was something they had never experienced or witnessed in their lives. Simply by being ourselves, regardless of the material covered, we were teaching, leading, and modeling a healthy, healing relationship. We were all healed because of it. The students witnessed what is possible for them and we came to see the depth of love just in being who we are. That is how we are meant to live. If we just breathe, live who we are and who we are becoming, in whatever context that feels right for us (the actual career or relationship is irrelevant), we are doing what we came here to do. This journey is not meant to be a struggle. We do, however, have an amazing ability to make it very complicated and convoluted. I tend to believe we do that in order to make it feel like a real success story when we work through an issue after much struggle and heartache. If we didn't have the struggle, would it really be a worthwhile achievement? That all depends upon your perspective. Thankfully, each year the school continues to evolve, as do I. It has been a wonderful experience and it continues.

While all this was going on, Mike seemed to be getting older each day. He got his driver's license, bought a used car, and gained some more freedom. Amy was moving through her college years and our lives were still so intertwined I loved it. Mike and I were going through that awkward period where he was becoming a man but he was still my son. Between Amy's junior and senior years of college, and Mike's junior and senior years of high school, the kids decided I needed time away. I was totally exhausted from all the hats I was wearing and all the responsibility they entailed. Somehow, in my humanity, I had lost sight of all the fun and simply identified with all the work. Around January, I had come home from work and collapsed. I somehow had managed to call Barb to ask for help just before I passed out. After an ambulance ride to the hospital with Mike, and with Barb and my mom in tow, it was decided that I was dehydrated, exhausted, and had pneumonia. A few days in the hospital made a world of difference and let me know how slack I had become in self-care. Teacher heal thyself! I made many changes in my life style and got stronger as the year progressed. By summer, however, Amy volunteered to come back to Connecticut to get a summer job and stay with Mike. Their dad lived 10-15 miles away in case, God forbid, there was a serious problem. I had so many girlfriends close by that they would be well covered. They had both consistently been on the honor role or the dean's list throughout their past few years and they were responsible, good kids. They were each working for the summer and they got along beautifully so I accepted. I considered a week in the Caribbean; they were thinking a month. They had no desire to lose me now.

I had never in my life taken more than a one week vacation so that was extremely outrageous. We had been team for a long time and they had no intention of changing that now. After collapsing into bed several nights in a row while this was in the back of my mind, I decided to seriously consider it. I am fully aware of the ramifications of pushing too hard and too long. I dealt with it with my clients every day and January showed I wasn't above it all. After running it by several friends, and looking at the general opinion, a friend pointed out that I was killing myself for the kids and that I had been a "phenomenal mother" giving endlessly all those years and it was now time to receive. That is a hard one to take in sometimes. Consequently, I needed to have it all affirmed again even after running it past a number of friends. We may know in our hearts and minds what is right for us but when it goes against everything we were raised to believe, no matter how much growth we have achieved, there are those times when we need that permission that comes from friends who can tell you how good a person you are and that you deserve it. All that took place just before the next life transforming experience was to happen. Soon after, I left for one month to go away to recuperate, replenish, and reclaim the me I had lost.

# Chapter Thirteen

## A Time for Me

*Sometimes when we have nothing left, life's
lessons bring new dreams to us.*

I HAD DECIDED TO SPEND MY TIME at Maho Bay on St. John's in the US
Virgin Islands. I spent a lot of time sleeping and regrouping. I read
a little and then sleep to the sounds of the beautiful tropical forest.
My days consisted of having a light breakfast in my room, taking a
cab ride to Solomon Beach for the day, and around 4:00 p.m. walking to the village for a salad and chicken, or, on occasion, a Roti
with a glass of wine. I would be back at my villa before 7:30, prepare for bed, and read a bit before sleep. Once I had caught up on
sleep, I had time to read, meditate, and just enjoy being alive. I was
then ready for more exploration. I enjoyed an underwater trail for
snorkeling and hiked from one village to the next for the exercise
and to see what else there was to see. It was all so beautiful with
such colorful little houses. The homes of the Caribbean certainly do
reflect the beauty and character of the place.

I soon grew restless, however, and I asked my cab driver where
he would go if he were to go off island and he said Anguilla. I had
never heard of it but he thought it was the most beautiful island in
the world. It turns out he came from there. I asked the regulars at
the beach I went to where they would go if they were to go off island and they all said St. Martin. I decided that with rave revues for
both places, they were both worth exploring and I now wanted an
adventure. I walked into the village, went to the travel agency there,
and asked for an open ended ticket to Anguilla and St. Martin. I had
once read something that said the worst risk is not to take one at

all. It was time to take a risk and grow some more. We are only as limited as we chose to be and I was ready for less limits.

The adventure began when I took a ferry to St. Thomas since there is no airport on St. John's. It felt so outrageous. Once I got to the airport, I checked in and waited for my 11:00 a.m. flight. The airport is so small you can see all the passengers come and go, regardless of the airline they are taking; it is one big room. As I sat there I watched the place fill up and empty, fill up and empty, again and again and again. I finally went to the ticket counter and asked if I had somehow not heard my flight called although I was really paying attention. As my introduction to the real Caribbean, since I was flying a local airline, the agent said to me, "Oh, you didn't miss it, your flight hasn't left yet. A man rented the plane and he's bringing it back when he finishes gambling in St. Maarten." My initial response, of course, was shock, "What did you just say???" It's amazing how anything out of our little box of experience just does not register initially. He couldn't have said what I just thought he said... Being intelligent, or so I thought, I asked again. I know he was thinking, "Yup, another tourist dealing with reality." Of course, the next "natural" question was, "You mean you let someone rent your plane when you already had scheduled passengers?" and of course, close behind, once it registered, "Are you telling me your airline has one plane?" Walking to Anguilla seemed like the next logical solution. This was a reality I clearly knew nothing about. What on earth had I done?

Here I was, thinking I was a big risk taker because I just walked into an agency and for $119 bought an open-ended, round-trip ticket to two other islands. Now I find out that was the easy part. I obviously looked a little flabbergasted since he suggested I go get myself a beer. He wasn't even going to give me complimentary drinks....... I had to sit down first. I noticed that three others had been sitting there with me while the crowds came and went. One woman appeared friendly so I approached her and asked if she was going to Anguilla and told her the story. She opted to get the beer. I am not a beer drinker so I got an ice cream and we sat on the curb just getting acquainted. She was from Australia but was working in a resort on St. Thomas and decided to take a couple days off to see a new island. Since she was living in the Caribbean, this was more of an inconvenience than a shock to her. Because I had no idea where I was staying (I figured I would ask at the airport when I arrived.), she suggested she get me a room with her discount at the same place she was staying so that we could share a taxi to the places we had each been advised to see. It sounded like a great plan.....

When we finally arrived in Anguilla (2 ice creams and 3 beers later) and went to our little hotel, it ended up we were right across the street from Johnno's, one of the recommended places which was a night club/restaurant on the beach. This was all looking up. We swam for the afternoon and then prepared to go out for a light dinner and then dancing for the evening. I stayed in the chosen hotel for that first night but planned on changing locations first thing the next morning. I had seen a beautiful villa I wanted to explore.

While I had been dancing that first night, I asked one man I was dancing with to tell me something about his island. He told me that as long as one man could fish, no one on Anguilla would go hungry. This truly sounded like the kind of community I had been looking for, for years. It sounded like the kind of community I had known as a child where everyone knew everyone. To confirm the impression I was getting, I asked someone else about the island and he said, "You don't need to like everyone here, but you need to live with everyone here." I was intrigued. The man I had danced with initially then introduced me to his circle of friends, men and women, and I felt so immediately welcomed in.

Anguillians are such a warm and welcoming people. Anguilla, itself, is a quiet, small, flat, arid island, 36 sq. miles in all, with a strong community pride. It also has 32 beautiful, if not exquisite, beaches of various size and attraction with coral and fish that can fill a day or week in snorkeling. I loved it. The other side of the smallness is that if you got a flat, if you needed help of any kind, anyone would stop in a minute and help you immediately. When you go out to do errands the whole trip is spent honking horns or flashing lights as so many people you know say hello in the local fashion. Many people don't have cars so simply standing along the road is an indication that a ride is needed for very young to very old. An expression I have used for years, "We are all in this one together" is truly the way it works there.

I had originally decided to spend 4 days on each island, Anguilla and St. Martin. I figured it gave me enough time to see each island and get back to reflect and relax for a couple of weeks before heading back to the states. So, I left Anguilla, with some regrets, to go to St. Martin. I had no idea if it was 3 hours away or 20 minutes away and I never thought to ask. It was another adventure and offered me more opportunity for exploration. This is such a glorious world, I wanted to see as much of it as possible even if Anguilla had been so wonderful. I certainly did not know that St. Martin was a 5 minute plane ride. It was right there. It was that beautiful island I had been staring at so often during my stay on Anguilla.

St. Martin/St. Maarten, although a small island, is part of two countries, French and Dutch on an island not much bigger than Anguilla. Because it is so very mountainous, however, it can hold almost 10 times the people by building up the sides of the mountains. Stories have it that one day, long ago, two men were left to walk from the outer points of the island and wherever they met, that would be the dividing marker of the two countries. It seemed to be the fairest way to divide one country into two. The Dutch side has casinos which are usually packed with both tourists and locals hoping for the big score. It also has extensive shopping and is English speaking which is a great help for many. The French side, St. Martin, is so very French. The streets are very narrow, the houses and shops are very close together, and the food is exquisite. The beaches are all clothing optional and still the clothing stores are filled. Nonetheless, after one day on St. Martin, I returned to St. John.

After being back on St. John for a few days, I really missed the beauty and warmth of Anguilla, both the people and the climate, along with the gorgeous beach of Shoal Bay. Coming over the rise and looking down on that blue-green water still causes my heart to take a leap. I wanted to return there—so I did. That same morning I went to the front desk, got back my unspent funds and caught a plane to Anguilla. After my first night at the original location with the woman I had met in St. Thomas, I moved to North Hill and stayed at Claudio Villas, built and owned by Ping Brooks. I called Ping and asked if there were any villas available, and thankfully there were. I was pretty much in shock at myself for a while. I had come to the Caribbean to recover, recuperate, get my energy back, and have much needed quiet time. Now that I had done all that, it was time for something different and so I moved to another island for the rest of my stay.

Never in my life would I have imagined myself doing such an independent, assertive thing. You know, sometimes it takes going away to another location to have the freedom to be who you really are. I know I had always made things happen for my children. I know I was immensely protective. Being strong and powerful was natural for me as a mother. It was required if I was to be the kind of mother I wanted to be, the kind of mother I had wanted. My ex-husband used to tell me the lions in the jungle had nothing on me when it came to protecting our young. I had even made the private practice and the Institute come alive, but it all felt as if those things were for the kids. They had nothing to do with me. Watching my own behavior now, like an outside observer, I had to own the fact that I was an independent, powerful woman who made things happen. It wasn't just for the kids, my clients, or family members; it was simply because that is who I am. That was quite a shock to own. How long can we deny what is obvious to everyone else?? Surprisingly long...

This bit of self-discovery changed things internally. I came to see myself differently and see my life differently. I had one more year left as a mom with a child at home. I was going to love it. Thank God for the gift of my children and thank God that they knew how loved they were. I used to ask if they knew they were loved since I never heard that as a child. They would laugh and say, "Ma, you always tell us, how could we not know?" They knew as well and with equal importance that I would always be there for them, loving them unconditionally. The greatest gift of this trip for me was the awareness that they loved me just as much. After my extended stay in Anguilla, I was renewed and ready to go home. I had come away and I found me, and them, on this trip. We had talked often, and depending upon who I was talking to, "Amy thought she was the boss" or "Mike was acting like a brat," but neither wanted me to come home before my time was up. I could also sense the love and humor involved since oftentimes we were all on the phone at the same time. I loved being a mom and I loved listening to them giving each other a hard time. It had so much love and understanding behind it. They could keep me in stitches. It was done lovingly. I would never allow brutality in my home ever again.

There is something other worldly about a mother's ability to hear the things that are not being said. I knew one would never squeal on the other but I knew they were hiding things and the fun of being a detective, or really playing hide and seek, and discovering who my children had become would begin as soon as I landed. I was honestly looking forward to it. When they were kids, they loved it when I discovered things they had tried to hide. They were in awe on occasion actually. They made it a challenge. They also plotted against me as well. When we were watching TV in the evening they would get me laughing so hard I would cry. They would keep pushing it and pushing it to see which one could make me wet my pants. It was a competition. If, and when, they succeeded, it just proved to them they could overpower Mom. They would go into hysterics and congratulate each other. They were in control. We were quite a group. I wanted to go home to my children, the ones I had raised from the time they were in my womb. I was so truly blessed. I was immensely grateful to them for this time away. I was grateful to Amy for her unselfishness in coming to Connecticut for her last summer and to Mike for understanding my need to recover and get another perspective. They were a mother's dream. Now I was going home to help each finish their last year of school, one from high school and one from college. I was fully aware that things would change soon, in a very big way. My dream, and intent, was to cherish every minute of this year if I could. I wanted to get all I could from the time I had left, claiming them as mine before others moved in and took them away and before we all became adults, instead of a mom with her little ones.

# Chapter Fourteen
# Their last year at home

*My Dreams for them and me*

WHEN I GOT HOME, I FELT I was prepared for the last year of having a daughter in college. She was becoming such a woman now; and, prepared for having my son in his final year of high school. I had never been away from the both of them for a whole month. He was getting so tall (He was finally taller than his sister and he made it clear he had waited his "whole life" to do that) and he was becoming such an adult in so many ways while still such a child in others. Mike was preparing for college, looking at schools, etc. and Amy was ready to stop studying. She just wanted out. I just wanted this to be a great year for all of us, since things would soon change.

I quickly discovered many of those things they hadn't mentioned on the phone. The party Mike had and the people Amy had confronted. They were a team and that was the most important thing of all. We were a family. We moved right into getting Amy ready for her last year of school with a 6 months supply of soap, shampoos, etc. Mike and I got the brochures and applications for a number of colleges. As we did with Amy, we picked a couple of reach schools (tougher to get into), a couple hopes, and a couple easy shots. I wrote the checks and he wrote the essays. Now we just had to wait until January. That month is sooo far away when you are waiting. This was my second time so I had a little patience, but nonetheless it seemed to take forever and the wait was just beginning...

With all this going on, I was receiving calls from my new friends in Anguilla inviting me to come for Carnival, which is similar to

Mardi Gras but so much more intimate. The kids said "Why not?" This was all so crazy. I had never taken more than a week off and now I had taken a month and NEVER before had I had two vacations in one year much less in one summer. If this was a new life style I loved it, but it took getting used to. Because we had accomplished so much in getting the kids ready, there wasn't much left to do. Somehow I had justified taking on a much larger mortgage because we were close to the kids' schools. I had justified private schools because I wanted them to have a great education but, still, justifying taking all this money for another trip for me took time. How many mothers can spend so readily on their kids but hesitate about spending on themselves? What a thing we do to ourselves... So I took off and went to Anguilla for Carnival and again stayed at Ping's. This trip gave me a much different feel for the island since now it was activities morning, noon, and night. There were boat races every day and activities in the village every night. I felt like a foreigner in some ways and as if I had come home in others. After the trip, I had come to really love the island and its people but I was looking forward to the year with the kids. I felt pulled in some ways. I had found a wonderful island and yet somehow wanted to blend all that in with my life in the states as a mom but had no idea how.

That last year of having a child at home can be so sentimental, so sad and yet so freeing. Again, so many seemingly contradictory emotions came up. I wanted them both at home yet I was looking forward to the idea of being alone, having a clean house all the time, freedom not to cook, and no worries each time he went out at night in his used car. It may be nature's way of preparing us to let go. I had already heard the stories of him driving fast. Somehow at college he may do all those things but I wouldn't know about them, specifically, so I wouldn't be so worried. As a result of his growing, and aging, we needed to continuously create new guidelines. I rarely said "No" to my kids. I didn't need to, but when I said "No" it was "No." He may not have liked my answer at times but my kids did respect what I said and he obeyed. I believe that if we, as parents, keep things simple and do not need to prove we are the parents, they already know and things go so much easier. Kids need freedom to find their own boundaries and they need freedom to make mistakes. If we are blessed, and they know they are loved, hopefully the boundaries and the mistakes will never be too seriously impactful.

I always gave my kids too much at Christmas but I loved that holiday. For Amy's last year of officially living at home, I asked what she wanted more than anything in the world. If I could afford it, she would get it. She thought about it and then said she wanted a week far away and for me to come with her. I went to my room and cried. I couldn't believe I was loved so much. How many kids ask that of a parent? We finally chose Cancun since it was supposed to be good for all ages. We did spend a fair amount of time together. It was a relaxing vacation for her, getting away from school, the cold, and her life, and a very touching one for me. After this it was downhill to graduation and her first nursing assignment and we had no idea where in the country she would go. It was all coming so quickly. I was so very grateful for this time together.

Mike had gotten into his first choice Cornell University. It was quite a dilemma for him. He is a ski racer so he wanted to race for Boston College where he was accepted also, but he wanted a major that Cornell was famous for. Although it was difficult for him to make the choice, I was thrilled for him to have been so affirmed. Before I had time to fully adjust to all this (I had been putting it off), all the preparation began. He was officially leaving home and I was officially losing my at-home family. Both of us were adjusting to the shift long before it took place. I had been through it with Amy. Mike was my baby, my last one. His leaving represented so much more. It was the end of a life stage, a rite of passage for us both.

We were moving into newer and newer arenas along this journey. My son, who had thought he was dumb because he had a reading tutor in the first grade, was now going to Cornell. He had made the honor role throughout the last two years of high school and was now getting the rewards. It was a difficult but warm and touching time for me. We spent a good part of this last summer looking at catalogs of college supplies. We had gone shopping for everything else that he would ever need in a dorm. I had not been a perfect mom but I had tried with everything I had to give. I had loved totally and unconditionally, with all of me. I think we can all look back and see things we would have done differently if we knew then what we know now, but we didn't know then. We had to work with what we knew. I would skip any mention of dirty rooms, I would have paid half for an inexpensive new car rather than have them driving around in old wrecks waiting to break down, and so many more things I would have changed about me.

When it was time for Mike to leave for college, I spent the morning shutting myself down emotionally to protect a breaking heart and to let him go more easily, for both our sakes. I had rented a van since we had so many things to bring with us. We were all set and ready for the long drive to Ithica, New York from Hartford, Connecticut. Once we got to the dorm, Mike decided to copy some other students and put his bed up on piles of cinder blocks so that his small refrigerator could fit under the bed. The rooms were so small considering all we had brought. We had enough things to furnish a small village. Mike had said he wanted candy to help him study; I bought 4 cases. This would be my last chance to nurture in this way. While making his bed with his new special sized sheets and comforter, I discovered his little white "puppy." It was the stuffed toy he had had since I brought him home from the hospital 18 years before. He was taking it to college and yet needed it hidden so all his new friends would never know the child I was leaving behind, only the man he was trying to be. I knew he could handle all this, I just didn't know if I could. My greatest dream for each of my children was that they would know they were gifts from God, and that they know they were loved totally. My dream had come true. Amy could accept, most of the time, that she was a love; Mike has had more trouble with it. He knows he is loved completely and totally, but because he isn't perfect, he thinks he is less special than he is. I pray that gets put in perspective.

After getting him settled, I sobbed the whole way home from Ithica. I know I had felt relief at times that this period was coming, but at that moment, all I felt was grief at the end of another cycle of life. I stopped about 1/3 of the way home to eat and get some hot tea. I needed to be still, to let him go, in the natural progression of life so that we both could go on from here. I know where Amy got her propensity for drama, I was living it..... I quieted down enough to simply cry, rather than sob, the rest of the way home. The headache had left and my stomach didn't hurt as much. Still, I was going home without my son.

Finally, I reached our house in West Hartford, this huge home I had bought so the kids could have friends over, so they could have a place close to school, and so they could live as I wanted them to in a diverse community. Now without them, this house felt so big, so empty and so lonely. As I sat in the kitchen, with a glass of wine in hand, I realized, fully, that now I was alone. Now I had to decide where I was going with the rest of my life. I knew the kids would always need me in some fashion, but I also knew they were moving on. They had been the center of my life for what seemed like forever. I was divorced when Mike was in the first grade and now he was in college.

I had wondered about remarriage, especially when they were young so that they would have a two parent family, but the opportunity or person never seemed right. I had learned that people marry for a number of different reasons but that none of them had been right for me. If I were to ever marry again, I would want it to be because I was madly in love with someone who was just as madly in love with me. It certainly would be different the second time around. So many years had passed, I had changed so much  - my wants and expectations were so different from when I was 23. John was a good person in many ways but we were so very different and our ability to love had been so different as well. Our expectations were from two different worlds. By now I had accepted that I may be alone for the rest of my life. Gratefully, I had recognized the importance of deep intimate friendships in my life, both male and female, and thankfully had been blessed with many.

While sitting there, in the kitchen, I remembered my dream of someday living in the Caribbean when the kids were gone. Well, they were gone. I was alone and I did not want to continue working 16-18 hours a day at 2-3 jobs. I wanted a completely different life style and an opportunity to experience life in a completely different way. I looked at some of my options, seeing fewer patients, selling the house and getting a nice apartment further in the city, and so many others. As I sat with that, I knew I just wanted out. I wanted to get away and start all over, slowly, with less stress, less demands on me, and more time. I wanted a fresh start someplace else. The Caribbean had warmth, sun, and the water, and it was so much more laid back. It just felt so right, maybe forever, maybe for a while. I would let that unfold. I had saved every penny I made at the school over the years for Mike's college so I only needed enough now to support me. I called a real estate agency and put the house on the market. I called from the office to notify all my clients that I would be leaving the country in three weeks and I called American Airlines for a one way ticket to Anguilla. I was now ready, or so I thought, to begin the next phase in my life. I remembered a dream and I was off to pursue it, but only after I spent a few weeks feeling Mike's absence, Amy's independent womanhood, and my aloneness.

# Chapter Fifteen
## Manifesting the Caribbean Dream

*Some dreams define themselves -*
*What happens when we forget the details.*

MOVING TO THE CARIBBEAN SYMBOLIZED BOTH AN ending and a beginning for me. One stage of my life, that I had loved, was over and the next was just beginning. The one thing I knew for certain was that I wanted a major life change. I needed one. This had been a dream and I trusted, as always, that in following my heart, things would work out. They always did. I had been told years ago that my life would entail many, many new beginnings. It was equated to a snake in the sense of shedding my skin and starting fresh each year. Being born in January, I must say it has felt like that at times. Amazingly, on one level I speak of wanting some security, some predictability, some routine in my life and I do, in a way. I also love travel, meeting people, having new experiences, and seeing so much of the world that I haven't seen. There must be a way to have both; I just hadn't figured it out yet. When I first thought of going to the Caribbean after my kids were gone, I never thought further than the sun, warmth, and a much more laid back lifestyle.

I landed in Anguilla, with a few suitcases full of my things, and I spent a few days at Ping's while I looked for a home. His villas rent on a short term basis, for tourists. I would no longer be a tourist, so I needed a more permanent location. In a place like Anguilla, you need to know people in order to find out what is available. Everything is word of mouth. Consequently, Ping and I spent days driving around asking everyone we knew what was available. One day I headed out alone, feeling confident, and found a place. I moved in two hours later and immediately started making plans on how I would fix it up and make it mine. I filled the fridge and the cabinets and made my list of things to bring back next time I went to the states. Now that I had a home, I went out to find acquaintances and a few good friends. I wanted both in my life.

I had rented a two bedroom home overlooking St. Martin and the Caribbean Sea. A shed out back which had been a small laundry area at one point in time was turned into my office. A new girl-friend gave me a couple of old desks which I sanded and painted bright green. I added shelves to the walls for books and supplies and I then included a statue I bought in St. Maarten of a 4' tall parrot which I spoke to on "those" days. I was forced to stop work each day by sundown since every slithering, crawling, and flying creature in creation loved to come in to visit at dark. I fixed the second bed-room for Mike who would be down on his first break. Whatever you have heard about roosters, do not believe it. Roosters are extremely competitive creatures who do not know how to tell time. I had 5-6 roosters in my yard that competed all night long to see who was the loudest, and who could go the longest and the most frequently. I never could tell who won. I do know, however, it was usually the one on the side of the house where my bedroom was.

In a short period of time, I would discover that in a country as small as Anguilla, everyone quickly gets to know you by the car that you drive. Consequently, whenever anyone spotted my car in the yard, whether at 6:00 am or 3:00 am they would stop in for a drink. I may not have told them where I lived, perhaps intentionally, but I didn't need to, my car spoke for itself. In the states, whenever any-one stopped by my house, I fed them. It may have been munchies, appetizers, or a meal, depending upon the time. It, however, always included food. Many Anguillians do not have the money to feed un-limited guests but rum is as cheap as it gets, so that is the equivalent.

There are some wonderful idiosyncrasies wherever you go, and we have ours here on Anguilla. Here all liquor is called rum. So when someone says, "I would love a glass of rum" I always ask what kind. They may mean vodka, brandy, one of the 6 most common brands of rum here, or even gin. It is all rum.

It didn't seem to take long to recognize so much of the beauty of the people and the culture and amazingly to acclimate without a great deal of trouble. I found at one point that it would take work to fit in within the culture of the states again, if I were ever to go back there to stay. I would go back on a trip and find, without my conscious awareness, my speech had changed somewhat, my expressions had changed, and my expectations were so different. Nature is one of our greatest gifts in a place like Anguilla from the gorgeous sea to the rainfall. When rain comes, everyone gets joyful; it means water in the cisterns. All our usable water is rain water. It runs off the roof, down a spout, and into the cistern under the house where it is stored to be used for all our water needs. No rain, no water, life is simple.

With all these differences, and apparent limitations, this was the beauty I had been searching for. Now that I had it, I found I did what so many do when they first get here after what feels like a long life. I slept, cried, read novels, and dealt with the shock that I had really done it. I had known I wanted something simpler, something so much less stressful than what I had been living. I needed a major change internally and externally and this was definitely major. I wondered if my timing had been right but I knew that I couldn't have done it any other way. I had nothing left to give. Now I was going to replenish, receive, and be filled.

I now had unlimited time, and the luxury, to look at my life, where I had come from, what I had been through, where I was, and where I wanted to go in detail, hoping to learn a lot from the self-exploration. I also looked at my marriage and again grieved. It seems grief can come up in stages. You think you have finished and then, out of nowhere, comes this grief again when you think, we were supposed to be doing this together. We were supposed to go through this transition together. We were supposed to be grateful we had raised these two beautiful children together. We were supposed to be grateful for this time to be alone again, to rediscover each other again, with all our joined history. Then I remembered my ex more clearly. He would never have done this. If he were to pack up and move anywhere, it would have been to a ski resort. That allowed the grieving to stop and me to move on. (Reality checks can be fantastic tools.) I would say it took a good six months to have it sink in that I had really done this. I was really here. I was really free. I had loved my life; I just needed something different now. It was time for a change. In the meantime, life went on.

Within one month of my settling in, the woman who was managing my business in the states decided to quit. She had realized she needed to work with someone beside her, not so far away. Now that I was gone, she didn't want the job anymore. Within one-half hour of hearing this news, I went from the panic "Oh my God, what have I done?" to the logic of "OK the next step in dealing with this problem should be...." to trust "Lord, we have a problem here. I need guidance, a good thought, something. If you have led me here for a reason, I trust you will resolve this problem" to faith "Lord it is in your hands." I knew if I was meant to be here, something would happen to bring all this to a great resolution. If I was here to do my ministry in another way, in a way that fed me and others, within a different context, then it would be taken care of. I truly believe that whatever we do, if it is in integrity, and it is an expression of who we are, it is our ministry. Literally, within a half-hour, a former student, Anne Murphy, called to say she was so excited about the news of my move. She said if there was ever anything she could do to help, she was more than willing. I asked if she wanted a job. (Where did that come from?) I was as shocked as she was. That was not what I would have thought of, but it was out now. She thought I was joking and started laughing. She had been teaching for 20 years and had just left. When she knew I was serious, she gasped and then accepted, and a wonderful supportive and life-giving friendship and partnership developed. I swear there is no such thing as coincidence. How many times have I said, "We never walk alone"? Looking back, I can see we were exactly what the other needed. Anne's love of people brought so many students into the school and allowed me to relax and be at home. I gave her a job she adored and that gave her so much of her life back, at a time when she needed it most. Our partnership worked well. I brought her down here a number of times to assist me in doing workshops and she loved it. It was one of those wonderful situations that are win-win.

Within the first few months, while managing my business in the states, adjusting to the self-image of having a full-time, on the books, employee, paying payroll taxes, etc and deciding to become an LLC, I was forced to look at my self-image as a single mom from the projects who had made it out. My past, although unconscious, was still so much a part of my life. I still carried a fear that had nothing to do with, and no acknowledgment of, what I had accomplished. Somehow, as with many women, there was a belief that you had been lucky, you had snuck under the ropes and gotten through, but if anyone found out you would be sent back to where you belonged. You have worked your butt off, you have raised your kids, and you have created a life. You have done it. It takes time, reflection, and self-appreciation to let that sink in; that was what I wanted to do now - let all that in. My fear didn't have to make sense to anyone else. Until I could let it go, I still lived under this cloud of having made it out, while holding a fear of going back.

Friendship was the one strong hold that I knew would allow me to keep perspective. About the time I moved here, Barbara packed up and moved to Arizona. We both followed our dream. Hers was to open a Healing Center Retreat House; mine was to hopefully lead a healthier lifestyle teaching and healing in an exotic setting. We had been such an important part of each other's lives, through raising the kids, divorces, career changes, graduate teaching at the same college, developing HSP skills, dating, weight gain and loss, personal growth, teaching at my Institute, and the loneliness of living. We did not want to lose that connection which we knew was a gift. To keep it going, every time I flew in from Anguilla to West Hartford, Barb flew in from Arizona. Around the time I sold my house, Barb and Annie sold theirs and so we all decided to get an apartment where Annie would live full time and Barb and I would live whenever we were in the states. We had joked for years about living together when we were older, but that was still decades away. We would be like the Golden Girls on the TV show. The only problem, however, was that we all wanted to be Blanch. On occasion, we could all see one or the other doing Rose really well, but Dorothy represented the responsible position we did not want - been there, done that, now was our chance to break out...

We couldn't tell if we had finally gotten it together, or, if we were just losing it and just didn't know it. (Which was quite possible) As long as there was laughter, we were willing to play. When we all got together in West Hartford, laughter was everywhere. It was like being kids again, having a long term sleep-over. We would all sit on the bed at night, once we were all home, and just laugh or cry with each other over what had happened since we were last together. When you have loved someone for years, you know their every quirk. You know their areas of insanity. You know their blind spots. You can see it coming when this poor soul is riding along thinking she is sailing high; you know where this is headed. Because of the choice to love, you sit and you wait and when she needs you, there are no fingers pointed, no "I knew it," you just hold her... and you understand. And boy, did we understand. The woman's story is the women's story, only the names change. Women can be a gift beyond words to each other if they allow it to happen and yet so many are so afraid of letting another in. We walk the same journey no matter how different the trappings look. We are all in this together. Letting go of judgment and self-righteousness makes us all equals and allows us to all be friends and mutual support systems for one another. We all need it. We need the laughter, the shared tears and the shared wisdom once the tears are over, so that our loved one perhaps will not walk into it again adding more pain. There were also all the shared congratulations, the shared pats on the backs for a job well done, or a relationship riding high, even if only for the moment. We never walk alone, unless we choose to, but, even then, there is the Holy Spirit walking beside you every step of the way. I have carried a prayer with me, in my pocketbook, for years, called FOOTPRINTS. It is well worn, even covered in plastic. It got me through those times when I didn't think I could go on. The author is unknown or I would surely share his or her name with you. For those of you who may not know it, it goes like this:

## FOOTPRINTS

One night a man had a dream. He dreamed he was walking along the beach with the LORD. Across the sky flashed scenes from his life. For each scene, he noticed two sets of footprints in the sand, one belonging to him, and the other to the LORD.

When the last scene of his life flashed before him, he looked back at the footprints in the sand. He noticed that many times along the path of his life there was only one set of footprints. He also noticed that it happened at the very lowest and saddest times in his life.

This really bothered him and he questioned the LORD about it. "LORD, you said that once I decided to follow you, you'd walk with me all the way. But I have noticed that during the most troublesome  times in my life, there is only one set of footprints. I don't understand why, when I needed you most, you would leave me."

The LORD replied, "My precious, precious child, I love you and I would never leave you. During those times of trial and suffering, when you see only one set of footprints; it was then that I was carrying you."

Anonymous

I was living in a new world, believing that I was here both because I needed and wanted to be, and also, because it was where I was led. In opening up to whatever would unfold, I did the basic prep work, I did my part. I applied for my work papers, which is a very involved and time consuming task. I ended up buying a new car. I got a little jeep since the roads here can destroy the underside of a car, and I bought the necessary items that turn a house into a home. I was really aware that I was starting out all over again. I had done this 20 years ago, beginning a business, making contacts, and watching my money. Now I was just doing it thousands of miles away and in a totally different environment. I wondered if life would always be a continuous process of starting over. I had always thought of myself as a self-starter but I had learned that I did not want to do everything all by myself again. It is lonely and so much harder. Some of the lessons we learn need to be integrated into our behavior and this was one of them for me.

I started dating again. I love to dance and in those days Johnno's was open 6 nights a week. The man I had met as a tourist proved to be a nice friend but not someone I would be involved with. Consequently, once I was out dancing I met another man who had asked me to dance. He was, and is, a beautiful dancer. When you love to dance, and do it well, there is a huge difference between those who know the steps and those who know how to dance. It is in the soul. This man danced with such confidence and joy he made it fun; he made dancing such a pleasure to anticipate. We met often and spent 4 months dancing, talking, and getting to know one another. After 4 months it seemed as if I knew him well. We had danced, gone out, gone on picnics, gone to St. Martin/St. Maarten on excursions, and had so much fun. I had met so many of his family members on both islands. One thing we did, and did often, was laugh. I had never laughed so much in any relationship I had ever been in. He was the most supportive man I had ever met. If anything needed to be done around the house, it was done within the hour. He loved being needed. I was really thrown for a loop by the idea that I had brought in such a gift. As a result, it seemed so right that we should become involved and so, after 4 months, we were.

Dak had taught me to own my power, to behave always as an equal partner, and to own my worth. Ansel taught me what it meant to be nurtured, to be treasured, and to be supported in every way. There was nothing he wouldn't do for me. We radiated when we were together. He grew and I softened and opened my heart, again. I didn't know if I could ever love again and I discovered I could. My marriage hadn't destroyed my ability to give so fully. I felt so loved, so light, and so wanted. It seemed to be everything I ever could have wanted or desired in a relationship. I had come so far. I had learned so much from my successes and my failures and I had brought all that into this relationship.

I was now beginning an adventure into a culture that made every naive, or denied, notion I had ever had about relationships come up front for me to look at. We were together for three and a half years. Most of that time was the most glorious, nurturing, affectionate, fun-filled, adventure-packed time of my life. I believe it was Spirit's way of letting me know what is possible. It was a gift I shall always treasure. I also felt blessed since I was getting to know the island, and the ways of the people in such a personal way. What I learned, unfortunately, is that even after receiving a diamond ring, seeing an architect and finalizing plans for our house, getting land surveyed and so on, and beginning preparations for marriage, I was not protected from the same fate as so many others. The man I was in love with, the man who wanted to marry me, wanted other women as well. I let him have them, all of them, full time.........

I was devastated. The pain, the betrayal, and the violation was beyond words. I had thought I could never love that way again but I had. Years before, I had been devastated when my marriage ended and had gone into a deep depression. Then, I wondered if I would survive. This time, I got angry. It is a much better response. It feels much more powerful and you do not become inactive. On the contrary, I became very active. I packed up all his things from throughout the house, including his bike, and delivered it all to his mother's. I was done and have stayed done. It took quite a while but I recovered. We need to know who we are and what we want. It is so much better to be alone than to be with someone who would willingly betray you or destroy your self-worth.

Alone, you still have friendships, platonic male relationships, your dignity, and your future. Most importantly, you still have you, and you are not living in self-betrayal convincing yourself and others that you are OK when you are dying inside. Life is meant to be lived, enjoyed, and relished. It is a gift and an adventure. Anything that causes you to simply survive is toxic. Thank God for the years, the wisdom, and the experience of living. They can all teach you so much if you are willing to learn. I relied on my self-knowledge, my experience, and the self-love I had worked so hard to develop and it worked.

Being out of a relationship makes life so much easier, and so much more complicated, no matter where you live. Being on Anguilla, however, I could go to the gym from 5:00-7:00am and then go for a swim in the glorious blue-green Caribbean Sea. When I am swimming the standard stroke, I can get lost in the rhythm that develops, when I swim on my back I get to stare at the beautiful clear sky and the surrounding hilltops. Inevitably, I go into awe thinking, "This is my life." I have truly been blessed. I am still learning and still growing. I know now that I am still capable of loving and loving fully, and maybe, someday, I will meet someone who is capable of loving in return, exclusively. I will wait. In the meantime there is still so much more to see and to learn and to explore.

Now that all my daily attention could go toward myself, my work, and my two cats, I had so much more energy to put into working. Thank God I love what I do. On Anguilla, I helped in the Community Welfare and Development Department when a psychologist was needed as well as developed a private practice at a new medical center on the island, Hughes Medical Center. I was also a staff writer for a local magazine doing a column called *JUST THINKING ABOUT*. I was also a writer for our weekly newspaper doing articles offering a psycho/spiritual perspective on things. I wrote two books *Dreams Are Only The Beginning: Becoming Who You were Meant to Be* and *The Companion Workbook* as well as creating a tape for relaxation and learning. I went back to the states 6 times a year for 10 days to teach at my Institute. While I was there I got to do TV shows and radio shows when asked, and also lectures or seminars during the week when not seeing patients since classes are only on the weekends. Somehow, I still feel, most days, as if life is just beginning. I am looking at what I want to do next.

I would love to develop more training programs and bring people to this beautiful island. My students are required to come here for one week, as a group, between their second and third years. The growth that takes place is enormous. I fully believe that going to a totally different environment encourages people to let go of their defenses and move much more quickly into the next step of their growth. My ministry, which started officially when I was in religious life, has gone through a series of transformations and yet is still about supporting others in their unending journey of spiritual discovery through joy, laughter, appreciation, and unconditional love. What better gift can I give?

For me, after almost ten years of living on Anguilla, it became time to create another dream. It was time to put it out there and ask for help, to ask the Holy Spirit for a clear message. By this point, however I wanted it written out, loud and clear. There should be some benefits, or short cuts, after spending so many years of service. I figure, if I got the message clearer, with some help, then I have more time to bring the message to those who are ready to hear it. I believe that in a relationship, even with God, there is meant to be a degree of mutuality and understanding. If my message is to spread the word of unconditional love and never walking alone, no matter where that is to be lived, I expect help, guidance, and humor along the way.

# Chapter Sixteen
## Taking it All to the Next Level

*Dreams can change even in the process of defining them:*
*New opportunities present themselves, some*
*should be chosen and some not.*

As always, when I put it out there, I get a response. When I mentioned in prayer that I wanted to know where I should go next, how I could best serve while enjoying the process of living my life, someone clearly was listening. One of my students asked if I would be a part of the Advisory Board of a multi-million dollar Frontier Medicine Grant the University of Connecticut had received from the National Institutes of Health (NIH). Shortly after accepting, I was asked to be Co-Chair of the Advisory Board. From there, I was awarded grant funding to research the work I had created, The W.I.S.E™ Method, in working with Fibromyalgia patients. I decided to use that research to complete a dissertation for doctoral studies. In addition, The University of Connecticut Medical School received a grant to offer classes in Complimentary and Alternative Medicine. I was asked to help teach Energy Medicine at the Medical School as a result of that grant. Talk about dreams… I was not permitted to go to nursing school since my high school was unaccredited and yet here I was teaching in a medical school. Truly miracles and the "impossible" can happen every day. If we let them.

With all of this happening, as well as my Institute being in a position of needing to grow or it would die, I decided, with mixed emotions, to go back to the United States to take my life and my work to the next level. I loved Anguilla, and I still do. I wanted to stay there forever, that had been my intent when I came, and yet at the same time I knew on a cellular level that it was time to recognize that I went there to heal and I had.

I went there to find me, a new way of life, and a new beginning. All that and so much more had been accomplished personally and professionally. Although a dream of mine is to build or buy a home there, both to call my own and to solidify my place in a land I love, it is clear to me that my work, my vision for my ministry, had grown and needed to expand. As a result, I was excited, scared, and glad to be going home to the states as much as I was sad and lonely at leaving what had become my home and my life. I found it amazing that I could belong to two places equally with such a deep heart and soul connection. The extent to which we can love, even a country, when we willingly open our hearts never ceases to amaze me.

Upon returning to the USA, there were many changes that needed to take place. I had rented a one bedroom apartment in the city during the previous two years, since Anne had moved away, and stayed there whenever I was in the states. Now I would live there temporarily as a means of getting to know this world again. It all felt so tight, so clean, and yet so lacking in fresh air and in life. I missed the outdoors, the water, the views of the Caribbean, and knowing almost everyone, and being known, no matter where I went. I was back in America, a larger and much more spread out country with so many circles to travel in and with no one really knowing others outside their small circle.

My focus turned to my school, The Institute of Healing Arts and Sciences, (IHAS). My return caused a lot of changes to take place. I had been the absentee owner and now I had returned. Watching the day-to-day operations forced me to see the strengths and weaknesses of the organization. I saw the immense talent and commitment of those who worked for the school as well as the things that needed to change if we were to go to the next level, whatever that meant. A level of growth, as with many dreams, requires immense inner and personal growth, and yet it also requires a great deal of external growth as well. If we were to expand, the infrastructure needed to be strengthened. We would need more people; we would need more things to be in place if we were to be able to grow. It seemed to be a logical next step although I was not too sure of what that meant or what it would entail. Exploring the process seemed to be the best way to find out. However, that meant letting some people go, hiring new people, reevaluating the curriculum, and reassessing our focus. Eventually, the changes began....

I added a two year program, which people had been asking for the past few years. They had wanted something that was less intense, and less demanding, yet which also caused them to grow and experience their life rather than survive it. In offering it, we found people actually wanted what we already had but without the work involved. You cannot grow without work, both in looking inward and in doing the outward changes necessary to be able to integrate the new you into your life. As a result, we eventually duplicated the curriculum that already existed yet offered it at different times, over more weekends but with less hours each weekend, permitting those with less flexible work hours to attend the Institute as well. We appealed to a wider audience.

My little school, my avocation, had become an institution. I had been the only teacher for years and now, at one point, I had 30 on our teaching staff. Because we were now affiliated with the Department of Higher Education here in Connecticut, I had a Director of Curriculum. At the insistence of the State, this new director, Faith Parsons, took what I had always taught and put it in a long manual for all teachers to follow so that the curriculum would then be consistent in every class. Because we were legally affiliated with almost 50 hospitals across the USA where my 3rd and 4th year students did medical internships, I also had a Director of the Internship Program along with preceptors who supervised all of our student-interns. My little program of 6-evening classes had been transformed. In the process, I couldn't help but notice that I had as well.

As our dreams get larger, as our vision expands to include so much more than we ever could have imagined, we are personally required to grow with them. We are required to develop the skills, the insight, the wisdom, and the vision needed to support our dreams coming into fruition. I have seen so many clients and students who want to dream big and yet who do not want to change at all. It is impossible. We need to grow to fit our dream. We need to have the ability to sustain it. Dreaming big requires becoming big ourselves, in our ability to love, to learn, and to manifest. Those who are called to be the visionaries of the world have had to grow beyond themselves. They have needed to see where their dream fits. They have needed to risk a great deal, and usually often, to accomplish their dreams. The price is as big as the dream. Rarely is the real price financial. Often it requires a new self-image, a new way of relating to people, a willingness to look at ourselves in the mirror, and to see all the strengths and weaknesses that exist there. Dreaming and following those dreams is not the same as fantasizing while lying on the beach. A dream may come from fantasy initially, yet when it becomes a dream for real, it is a calling from our soul to become so much more than we are right now. It is a call to become who we were meant to be; sometimes one step at a time and sometimes by taking one giant leap off one cliff after another. When we realize the level of freedom we have achieved, the level of passion, vibrancy, and aliveness that is available within us, we can't imagine not doing it. We come to recognize that before each leap, we are required to let go of one more thing, one more part of ourselves that may have been holding us back, perhaps a poor self image, a belief in our inadequacy, a fear of failing, a fear of succeeding, or even a fear of being seen. What we let go of can be different for each of us but the need to let go and to hold onto something else is not.

Years ago I could not have imagined ever letting go of one piece of IHAS, one aspect of who we were and where we were going. I have come to see that at some point, a business requires so much more than any one person can provide. I needed more assistance, more support, and more collaboration than ever before. I was not the same person I had been when I founded IHAS and consequently IHAS now needed to change to reflect who I had become. Who I was in this context, and how that was to be reflected, really was the question. I did not have a clear answer. If I was going to go for licensure to bring this company and the field of energy medicine into the mainstream, if I was going to take the message I have been teaching for 16 years to a larger audience, one that is hungry for this message, it would require more than I could provide alone. I had hired a phenomenal staff, and now we were moving forward even further and possibly becoming a public holding company, a recommendation made by a business consultant I had hired who was highly recommended by others in the Hartford business community. For a girl from the projects who never knew what a stock was, I would now possibly be the President and CEO of a stock holding company. This was a dream beyond any expectation I have ever had or even imagined. Dreams are like that. While you are focusing on one, others develop from that. They build on each other and allow you to see that those increments are needed and probably guided and put in place by others. Without faith that we are being led by Spirit, I don't know that I ever could have taken these risks, these leaps of faith. They are more than I ever imagined.

As with all dreamers, I had people who said, "That is ridiculous. You are too small a company. You have no idea what you are getting into. You have no idea of the cost or of the liability. Don't do it." I also had others who said, "God, are you brave. Go for it. What a great turn of events. It will be great for you and the company. I want in." It is a solid reminder that always there are those who say "Run" and those who say "Fly." I want to fly. Forming a public holding company is a scary and exciting thought. Before making that decision I needed to take the time to look at my life. I needed to remember that all along the way, there have been others who have questioned my ability and my dreams, and there have always been those as well who admired my skills, my courage, and my willingness to take a risk. Consistently, which group I choose to listen to is up to me. What I know for a fact is that I have always landed on my feet. I have not always liked where I landed but if that was the case, I was only there temporarily. A new dream would develop, a deeper level of self-awareness would arise, and I would continue on with the journey on a path I may never have developed if I hadn't landed where I did. Each dream has lead to the next as dreams do. Each has helped me develop a strength I would need for the next one, even before I knew it existed. Unless you begin that first dream, you will never know where it could lead. I have found that there is some logic involved, but not much. It just happens. It unfolds and your choice is whether or not to follow it, whether or not to risk coming alive even further, to stop growing, or to grow on a different path.

In making the decision to pursue becoming incorporated, in placing all my trust in another's expertise, even a highly-recommended business consultant, in becoming a stock-holding company, I realized that the price was too high. The consultant had disappeared overnight, the promised investors never materialized, and my company had been redirected to a path I couldn't and wouldn't follow. We had been recently programmed to become "big business." When I took time out to reevaluate, what I saw was that my intent, my students, and my inner-peace were getting lost. My debt was increasing, and my joy was decreasing. I found I was spending each day in front of a computer, from early morning to long after everyone had left the office. What had fed me, the human interaction, the spiritual energy, the intimacy of watching my and others' spiritual growth, had disappeared. My job had become one of managing a company, of pragmatically guiding it, attending meetings, and making decisions all day but implementing none of them. Those opportunities for joy and creativity went to the staff.

Somewhere in the process I had gotten lost. I reassessed this new vision and wondered who it belonged to, where it had come from, and how I had let it develop. Somewhere in there I had lost sight of my own vision, I had lost sight of what the school meant to me, and I had allowed myself to be pulled into others visions, visions that didn't fit my personality, my gifts, or even my dreams. How often do we do that? How often do you let yourself be persuaded to follow another's dreams? If they are good at it, they can convince you it is your dream. At some point, without recognizing when, you lose sight of you and where you want to go with your life. When you finally realize what has happened, you need to reassess. Perhaps your dreams have changed without your knowing it; perhaps you were led to where you belong by someone who could see you more clearly than even you could. At other times, however, losing your dream and allowing yourself to be led by another can be a form of self-abandonment. What I learned in this reassessment was that bigger is not better for me. I truly wanted to lead people back to the truth of who they were, back to their soul's longings, and I wanted to remind people that they are the gift they bring to themselves and to others, but doing it through a bigger business model was not my way.

None of this was being lived while I spent my days and nights behind a computer, while I worked to be the chief administrator of a corporation. Knowing our strengths and limitations is a gift we give ourselves and those who work and live with us. On one level, I would have loved to see IHAS partnering with Hospice, locally and nationally, with the Visiting Nurses Association, and the American Cancer Society, as well as with all those who practice any aspect of medical care, so that we could support the practitioners in their own self-care and healing, while also supporting them in being fed in their patient interactions rather than being stressed or drained as has become the norm. Patients and those actively practicing health maintenance would benefit immensely from understanding the whole picture of health. Understanding how our personality affects our health and how our passion and vibrancy support our immune system is intrinsically important to self-care. I want the whole world to learn that, but how I teach that is where the decision-making process needs to come into play at this point. I could no longer do it in the context of an institution that I owned and managed and, as a result, this dream, this institute, needed to end. Knowing when to let go of a dream, when to move onto the next, can be immensely difficult. The value of taking a break, or reevaluating your life, and doing the inner work of self-discovery cannot be overstated at these times.  Going back to your truth is the only way to go forward and I needed to do that.

How could I tell people to live in their truth if I wasn't? How could I share the joy of life when I had lost mine? Another step, another adventure was coming, I could feel it. There is a reason for everything, including this process; I simply needed to look at what I had learned and where I needed to grow to make the move forward that was much more me and that much more real. I was getting ready for the next dream. It was clear that I now needed to learn new lessons, develop new skills, and walk, one step at a time, into the next stage of my life, while I also remembered that some dreams and some opportunities are not meant to be followed and most certainly when they lead us away from ourselves. We don't always recognize that, however, until after it has happened. Once we do, the next dream needs to come forward and my thoughts were spinning as to what that would be.

With all the emphasis on the Institute, one unrelated yet wonderful awareness I had achieved was that although I needed most importantly to live in the truth of who I was, I had also recognized that I did not want to do it alone. Not coincidently, as I started to reevaluate my future, I received an email from a man I mentioned much earlier. Ray, the man I had fallen in love with while in high school, the man who had taught me to dream, to love, and who encouraged me to risk, the man my mother forced me to break from, had been looking for me for many, many years. After many failed attempts elsewhere, through Classmates.com, of all places, he found me. We were both enrolled for a short period of time, and he happened to look me up a few weeks before my time was to expire.

If you recall, I had seen him after we were forced apart while I was on vacation in religious life, 4-5 years after entering. My father had taken me to see his parents' new home. His parents had loved me, and I them. Our two fathers had planned that I would see their home as soon as I had days free from the demands of religious life. During the visit his parents were as loving as always. As I sat in their living room, in my long black habit, having tea, Ray's mother had gone into the kitchen and invited Ray, his wife of one year, and their new infant to dinner. Ray walked in and saw me and his facial expression was dramatic. I thought he was enraged; in fact, he was in shock. I left his parents' home within minutes because of the shock of seeing him, seeing his new family, and feeling a world of emotions that were now unfamiliar. With one phone call, all those memories and more came flooding back.

After I responded to his email, we spent a month talking - for hours every evening. He is no longer married and we have now spent much of the last few months together, seeing each other almost every other week, flying back and forth from Connecticut to Florida. The joy, the smiles, the laughter, the exploration, the talking, and the love remain. We have met each others' children and grandchildren. Instead of 10 children of our own, we now have a combined total of 10 grandchildren and five children. He has been immensely successful in his own field, we have both had full lives and other relationships, and yet it feels like yesterday since we were together since there is a comfort, a familiarity, and a shared dream still. It is like coming home, back to where we belong. He still supports my every dream as I do his.

How will all of this translate into our daily lives? Into my work? In the long run, will this simply be a wonderful gift of finding a new/old friend? Will it become a lifelong relationship? Only time will tell where it is going. I only pray we both remain open to whatever the future holds naturally and that we each live, whatever this is, to the fullest. We deserve it. In the meantime for each of us, the joy of living, the blessing of taking the risk to love again, of living life fully, and of following all of our dreams, makes so much possible. Choosing to live, not to survive, provides the energy needed to take life to the next level. It also provides more and more opportunities to confront the next level of risks and the next level of self-awareness. This is not a decision you make once, however. You must make the decision to live fully and to take risks, again and again.

For me, the questions that arise are, "Will all this add to how I bring my message to the world?" "Will it open up opportunities that may have been closed previously?" "What will this change bring?" As always, having the answers makes life appear easier yet we rarely do. More than once I have said, "Lord, just show me what is coming. I can wait if I know what is coming." - or - "Lord, just a hint..."Yet as always, I only know when the time is right.

I keep reminding myself that without fear, there is no need for courage. I therefore am a very courageous soul but one with a dream, and a dream that keeps on growing and changing as do I. I have no clue as to how it will end but I do believe fully that we do not go home to Spirit until we have completed what we have come here to do. It seems I may be here for a very long time and I wish the same for you.......

God Bless

# Epilogue

None of us knows exactly how our lives will go. Some may have a better idea than others of how it is supposed to go, if they have a long family history that follows similar paths or responsibilities, but the future is always in our hands. Your present is in your own hands as well. You have already chosen your past but the rest is wide open. The past is like a school book you should read and come to understand, then let go of. Living in this day, this moment, and getting the most from it, is your present, your gift, to yourself. It is a wonderful idea to spend time at the end of each day looking at ways in which you supported your truth and your essence during that day, as well as observing the ways in which you chose self-betrayal. By reviewing how you have lived each day you are in, you can come to understand your greatest fears as well as have the opportunity to own your greatest strengths. Your life is right there for you to look at....

You can come to see that life is so much more than just getting by, than just pushing forward. You come to see that it is an unfolding story. Just as any director or producer might, you have the freedom to change a few scenes in tomorrow's filming. Has something that has happened today, or a realization that you have achieved, called for you to respond differently than planned, or even to change your plans? By taking the time to slow down and stop each evening, you can break a pattern of running and/or of reacting. You can bring YOU back into your life. You also give yourself the time needed to dream and to reach for the stars, whatever that means to you.

Through those dreams, you come to see all that you are capable of becoming, one dream at a time. They are all a gift you give yourself and, in truth, a gift you give the world. If we have each come in to make this world a better place, a holier place, then it is through our dreaming that we will make that happen. No one can dream your dreams; no one can make them happen except you. They are your gift and your responsibility to yourself and to the world. No dream is too big or too small; some simply take more time than others. Who knows, by the time it is ready to be completed you may have outgrown it and will then be ready for the next step, the next dream. Growth does that....

My children have now created their dreams, not their first, and God willing, not their last. Each has learned that there is nothing to lose in trying, in reaching for the stars, even when all others say "it cannot be done," "it is impossible," or, strangely, "it has never been done before." What a perfect reason TO do it. Progress and growth ONLY come when you do what has never been done before, or in a way it has never been done before. Another's fears have held so many, many back when they were called to go forward. If you don't have others to create fears for you, you can create your own if you really need them to justify staying still. That is a life choice.

My wish for all who walk this planet is that you reach within yourself to discover what it is that gives you life. In that knowing and in that fulfilling, the next dream can come alive. It is an adventure you have come here to live. Dreams, whatever your dreams, are only the beginning. They are the beacons that call you forward to continue becoming more and more of who you truly are. With that beacon, and the Holy Spirit by your side, you are ready to go forward into your future, living every one of your dreams even those you do not know you have....................

GOD BLESS